366
Stories for Bedtime

This edition published in 1984 by
Gallery Books,
an imprint of W. H. Smith Publishers Inc.
112 Madison Avenue
New York City 10016

Reprinted 1985, 1986

ISBN 0 8317 8500 4

Printed in Yugoslavia
by MK

366
Stories for
Bedtime

GALLERY BOOKS
An Imprint of W. H. Smith Publishers Inc.
112 Madison Avenue
New York City 10016

1 January
Happy New Year!

'Mummy, what's a New Year resolution?' Claire asked one day, when she heard her parents talking about it.

'You make a New Year resolution when you decide to do something good for a whole year, or, if you decide to stop doing something bad for a whole year,' explained Mummy. 'But you have to decide on New Year's Day, and that's today – the first of January!'

Soon she heard Claire talking to the cat in her bedroom, and crept close to listen: 'Tibs, you're not going to catch birds for a year, and then I won't smack you for a year.'

Two good resolutions, thought Mummy.

2 January
Pongo's neighbour

Pongo was a dog who was always boasting.

'Do you know,' said Pongo, to Dick the neighbour's dog, 'my kennel is as big and grand as a palace!'

'Could I come and see it?' asked Dick, who wasn't sure what a palace was. So the two dogs trotted off to Pongo's kennel.

It certainly was roomy and comfortable.

'My word!' exclaimed Dick, enviously. 'You are lucky to have such a grand home.' He wished he could think of some way to get even with Pongo. Suddenly, Dick caught sight of a large, juicy-looking bone in the corner. This gave him an idea.

'There goes your doorbell,' he said.

'I didn't hear anything,' said Pongo.

'I'm sure I heard it,' said Dick.

Pongo prided himself on being a good watchdog, so he hurried off, barking loudly.

When Pongo returned to say there was no one at the door, he found no one in his kennel – and no bone either! Poor Pongo.

3 January
Frederick's toys

'Surely you're not leaving your toys on the floor all night?' said Frederick's mother, when she saw the muddle in his bedroom. 'What a lazy boy you are!' But Frederick took no notice, and got straight into bed. He lay awake for a while thinking about his toys.

Suddenly, the room was in a turmoil. The fire engine was racing across the room, its siren blaring. 'Ow! Oo! Ouch!' howled the teddy bear, clutching his right paw, which had just been run over by the tipper truck. CRASH! went the house of bricks as it all tumbled down.

'Stop!' Frederick called out in a panic. 'Please be good! From now on I promise I shall always put you away at night.'

When Frederick woke in the morning, his room was quiet. He wondered whether it was all a dream, but he kept his promise.

4 January
A most unusual morning

When Isobel woke up, she felt in her bones that something was different. She jumped out of bed and ran to the window. Outside, everything had changed. The ground was covered with a thick blanket of snow, which hid the path, the flower-beds and the grass. There was no wind to blow the snow off the trees.

'Where are the birds?' she wondered. 'They're usually flying about and chirping by the time I wake up.'

Isobel watched the fiery red sun as it rose above the horizon. She wondered whether it was red with anger, because it had not been able to wake the world.

A bird flew on to the branch of a tree, making a shower of snow fall. It chirped, and Isobel laughed. She ran to tell her mother about this most unusual morning.

5 January
The little parakeet

Nina had been given the loveliest birthday present, and a most talkative one too – it was a brightly coloured parakeet. The little girl called him Peeka. She never grew tired of watching him pulling faces at his own reflection, and tapping with his beak at the tiny mirror.

But it wasn't long before he became rather lonely. He refused his food, and spent hours in the corner of his cage, with his head tucked under his wing.

Nina felt very sorry for Peeka. She made a big decision and took all the money out of her piggy-bank. She went to the pet shop and chose a companion for him.

Nina put the new bird into the cage with Peeka, and said, 'Cheer up, Peeka, here's a friend, called Boo!'

Peeka and Boo were very happy together, playing and chattering, which made Nina happy too.

9

6 January
Princess Cecilia

When Princess Cecilia was nearly twenty years old, her parents decided it was time she got married. So they invited all the handsome young princes and nobles whom they knew to come to Cecilia's birthday party. But the trouble was she couldn't make up her mind which one she wanted to marry.

Then she had an idea; she asked to see the royal pastry-cook, and ordered a specially large cake to be baked for the following day. But before the cake was put into the oven, Cecilia dropped her gold ring into the mixture.

Next day, when they all sat down to eat, she cut the cake up into pieces. When the lucky one found the ring in his slice of cake, he slipped it on her finger.

And so the pair were married; and each year afterwards, on their wedding anniversary, a special cake was baked – with a ring in it!

7 January
Skating

The snow falls like swan's down,
  So fluffy and white;
And when the sun's shining,
  It all looks so bright!
I'd like to go skating,
  Down there, on the lake;
I'm *sure* I can do it,
  If my hand you'll take . . .

8 January
Where's the snow?

It was a most unusual year. It should have been snowing by now, the countryside covered with a soft white blanket.

But this year there were no snowball fights, no sliding on the ice – just a clear blue sky and a bright sun that could not warm the freezing air.

Veronica felt disappointed as she put on her thick sweater, her woollen mittens and her knitted hat to go out for a walk. She would much rather have been building a snowman or skating on the pond. But you can't build a snowman without snow and you can't skate without ice.

Outside everything looked clear and bright in the crisp morning sunshine. The birds were singing, and in the field the pony pawed at the hard earth. He whinnied 'hello' as she passed, but then started back in amazement when he saw his breath float away like smoke.

Veronica laughed out loud and clapped her hands with pleasure. Who needed snow? It was a beautiful day!

9 January
The latecomer

Tap! Tap! Tap!

Mummy walked over to the window, to see what was making that quiet tapping sound.

It was Pippo, the nightingale. He had found the bird tray quite bare, and had come to ask for food.

'You're late today, Pippo,' said Mummy, as he flew over to the tray, perching hopefully on the rim. 'I put some bread crumbs out earlier, and some lumps of fat – but they've all been eaten.' She could see many birds' footprints in the snow.

'Here's something for you,' said Mummy, crumbling some bread over the tray.

Pippo trilled his thank you, and pecked up the crumbs quickly, to make sure no other bird got them. Next morning, he would get up earlier!

10 January
Skiing is easy

Claude, the kitten decided to spend his winter holiday in the mountains. He wanted to learn how to ski.

'It's easy,' he told his mother. 'I've seen pictures of people skiing, in my picture book.'

He was frightened when the cable-car swung him high into the air, over the ski-slopes and even over the tree-tops.

He climbed out at the top, fastened on his skis, and took a deep breath.

He pushed off gently, and started to glide smoothly downhill. 'Hooray!' he shouted. 'I'm skiing! Watch, everybody!'

Faster and faster he went, until he came to a bend.

Whoops! Claude's skis slipped away from under him, and he fell down into the snow. Luckily it was soft, and he didn't hurt himself. He stood up very slowly and carefully, using his ski-sticks, but . . . WHAM! Down he went again, flat on his back.

'Maybe I should have some lessons,' he thought. 'Skiing isn't easy after all!'

11 January
The silly snowman

Bridget had built a fine snowman in the afternoon, with a hat and a scarf to help keep him warm. But by the evening he started to grumble.

'Brrr . . . I'm cold,' he muttered. 'I'll climb up that ladder, and go and sit by the chimney for a while, and warm myself.'

Bridget was asleep in bed, and no one saw a white figure shuffling across the garden and heaving itself on to the roof.

'Ah! That's better,' smiled the snowman as he began to feel warmer. But his smile drooped at the corners, as he felt the soles of his feet turn to water. He slithered down the roof and fell with a soft swoosh and a thud into the garden below. He slowly shuffled back, to his old place.

Silly snowman! He never tried to move again.

12 January
Winter

Outside the snow is falling
   The wind is calling.
In front of the fire
   The cat rolls herself into a sleepy ball;
The dog growls softly in a doggy dream.
   The yellow canary is asleep in his cage,
All fluffed up on the perch.
   The goldfish, motionless in her bowl,
Blows lazy bubbles.
   Tick-tock, tick-tock,
Sings the old grandfather clock.
   Her nose pressed against the cold pane,
Stephanie watches the white flakes,
   Drifting, spinning, dancing down.
Outside the snow is falling,
   The wind is calling.

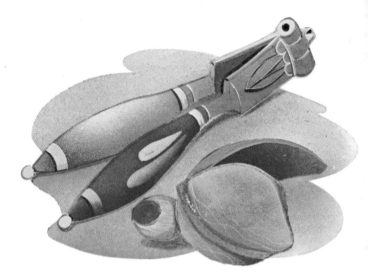

13 January
The nutcrackers

Whenever Simon visited his grandmother, he always went straight to the dresser, where his favourite plaything was kept. It was a pair of old nutcrackers, beautifully carved and painted.

'Do be careful with them, dear,' said his grandmother. 'They belonged to my grandfather, and they're very precious.'

One day, Simon went to play with the nutcrackers as usual. He picked them up, and one of the handles fell off. Simon was very upset, but he didn't dare tell anyone, so he hid them behind a book.

Next day, his grandmother came to see him.

'Don't worry, Simon,' she said. 'I knocked the nutcrackers on to the floor and broke them, not you! But you should always tell a grown-up if you think you've done something wrong.'

14 January
The red umbrella

Lucy had a red silk umbrella, which spent most of its time in a blue china umbrella stand, in the hall. Next to the red umbrella stood a walking stick.

'You're lucky,' said the red umbrella to the walking stick. 'You've been taken out for a walk every day this week, and I haven't been out once!'

'That's because the sun has been shining,' explained the walking stick. 'My master only likes going for walks when the weather is fine, and you go out when it's raining.'

'When Lucy went shopping with her Mummy last week, she took me with her,' said the red umbrella, 'but she never put me up! I stayed the whole time in the bottom of the shopping bag. Oh dear, when will I be able to stretch out my stiff arms, and feel the lovely cool, clean rain splashing all over me?'

Just then Lucy ran into the hall, wearing her raincoat and gumboots.

'Come on, umbrella!' said Lucy. 'It's raining, and you and I are going out!'

15 January
Jake's surprise

For several days now, Jake, the duck who lived at the farm, had not been able to visit his friends on the nearby pond. The weather had been too cold and grey.

But one morning a pale sun showed its face, and Jake decided to go down to the pond and have a swim with his friends. When he arrived, no one was there except for an owl, perched on a willow tree. The pond was very still and looked quite strange to Jake, but he didn't know why.

'Whoo-hoo-hoo!' said the owl. 'Jack Frost has paid us a visit, and left his looking-glass behind . . .'

'What is that silly owl hooting about?' thought Jake. 'He always talks in riddles!' He waddled quickly down to the edge of the pond and pushed himself off.

'Quack! Quack! What's happened?' shouted Jake in amazement, as he slid across the pond, landing on his tail with his little webbed feet waving in the air.

'Whoo-hoo-hoo! I warned you!' The owl hooted at him.

Did you understand what the owl meant?

The dolls' dresses

'I'm bored,' grumbled Genevieve, staring out of the window.

'And I've nothing more to read; what shall we do?' said Annabel, with a sigh.

'Come along, children!' said their grandmother. 'We'll have a competition. You see these two pretty pieces of material. Here are two pairs of scissors, needles and thread; the first one to finish making a dress for her doll will get a prize.'

'What sort of prize?' asked Genevieve.

'Quick! Pass me the scissors,' said Annabel. 'I'm going to lay my doll on top of the material, so I cut the dress out the right size.'

'I'm going to do that too,' said Genevieve, who was younger than Annabel. 'Granny, please thread my needle for me.'

The two girls happily snipped, pinned and sewed away, without a thought for anything else but the beautiful dresses they were making – and the prize they might win.

Annabel finished first, but Genevieve was so close behind that Granny gave them each a prize – a blue sewing bag, and a red sewing bag.

17 January
The little rabbit

Peter had been working hard at school, and had learnt to read. His father was very pleased, and gave him a present – a pet rabbit.

'I shall call you Twitchet,' said Peter, stroking the rabbit's ears, 'and you shall hop about wherever you like, and sleep on my bed at night.'

'Rabbits aren't like cats or dogs, you know,' said Peter's mother, looking worried. 'They chew things, and they don't have very clean habits; Twitchet ought to live in a hutch.'

'Oh, *please*, Mummy, give him a chance,' begged Peter; so his parents agreed.

Next morning, Peter couldn't find Twitchet anywhere. He wasn't on the bed, or anywhere in the bedroom. Peter slept with his door ajar, so he looked in the passage.

Suddenly, he heard his father say in a loud, cross voice, 'That rabbit has chewed the electric light flex!'

'And he's nibbled the corner of my book,' said Peter in dismay. After that, Twitchet lived in a comfortable hutch, and only came out on special occasions.

17

18 January
Nino has toothache

One morning, Nino the little elf woke up in a bad mood because he had toothache. He sat holding his cheek.

'What's the matter, Nino?' a rose bush called across to him.

Nino sighed. 'I have toothache, but I'm too scared to go to the dentist. You are lucky not having teeth.'

'But my roots sometimes get very dry and uncomfortable, which makes my leaves droop,' said the rosebush. 'Then the gardener waters me, and I feel better again. *And* he cuts off my dead flowers, to help me grow new buds.'

Nino was very impressed by what the rose bush had told him. 'Maybe my teeth will grow stronger if I let the dentist take care of them,' he thought, as he hurried off to have his sore tooth seen to.

19 January
The king's horse

There once was a king,
  Who had everything;
But he wanted his horse
  To be special, of course.
So they carved one of wood,
  Which made him shout, 'Good!
That's a very fine horse,
  For it's special, of course.'
But on his first ride,
  He slid off . . . and cried!

20 January
The new baby-sitter

Miss Owl lived in the forest, in a beautiful little tree-house. But she lived all alone, which often made her feel sad and lonely.

Now Mrs Squirrel, who lived in the tree next to Miss Owl, decided to invite her in to tea one day, with her friends Mrs Rabbit and Mrs Mouse. The baby rabbits and mice came too, and had a lovely time playing hide-and-seek. The mothers all chatted together, swopping recipes and stories about their children.

But Miss Owl had no such stories to tell, so she said nothing, and looked sad.

After a while, kindly Mrs Squirrel had an idea. 'We three must find food for our families,' she said. 'Would you stay and look after our children, Miss Owl?'

'Of course I will!' said Miss Owl, pleased to do something for someone else. After that, she often came to baby-sit.

21 January
The forgetful squirrel

Caspar the squirrel was very puzzled. He had spent a long time in the autumn collecting seeds and nuts, and hiding them away in the hollows of old trees.

Now it was winter, and he was hungry. But could he remember where he had left his nuts? No!

'Oh dear,' he thought, as he rested on a branch, watching Woody, the woodpecker, tapping away with his long sharp beak at a rotten stump. 'I hid my stores too well, and they will never be found.'

What he didn't know, was that Woody's sharp eyes had already spotted several of Caspar's larders. The greedy bird quickly gobbled up what was in them.

Caspar took up the search again – up and down, here and there, still with no success. Now he badly wanted food.

'I'll go and raid the bird table,' he decided. He was lucky, for there was a large crust, which he took away.

Do you think he ever found any of his nuts and seeds again?

22 January
The oak tree

It was a cold, fine day, and Amanda asked her father if she could go and play under the oak tree at the bottom of the garden. It was her favourite place for playing at teddy bears' picnics in summertime, but now, of course, it was winter.

Amanda's father helped her to put on her warm boots, bonnet, and away she ran, with Big Bear and Honey Bear in her arms.

But very soon she was back again, crying, and calling out, 'Daddy! The tree's dead!'

They went together to look at the tree.

'It's not dead; it's having a sleep – rather as we do, when we go to bed at night! In spring it will grow leaves again.'

'I wish it was spring now,' said Amanda. 'Come on, teddies! We'll have tea inside today.' She was smiling again.

23 January
The two kittens

Kelly and Kitty were two fluffy little kittens with brown and rust-coloured markings. One day, they decided to run off into the vegetable garden to look for an adventure.

They played together for a while, and then it started to rain.

'Oh no!' wailed Kitty, 'We'll get soaked if we run all the way back to the house.'

You know how cats hate to get wet, so they looked for somewhere to shelter.

'Quick! Let's creep under that big cabbage,' said Kelly; they both managed to wriggle under the lower leaves.

But Kitty started back in fright, as something landed in front of her nose, and waved its head to and fro at her.

'Run for your life! It's a dragon!' squeaked Kitty, and together they dashed back, wet through, to tell their mother.

'That wasn't a dragon – that was a caterpillar, and you disturbed him in his home,' said their mother, licking them dry again.

24 January
The happy orphan

Peppi was a pheasant. The farmer's wife had found him wandering about at the edge of a wood one morning, when he was only a tiny chick. She had a good look all round, but she could see no sign of the parent birds, or any brothers and sisters. So she carried him gently home, made him a cosy nest with some rags in a basket near the oven, and fed him.

Soon, Peppi behaved as though the farmer's wife was his mother! He followed her around, perched on her shoulder, and helped himself to food from her plate.

When he was fully grown, with long, brightly-coloured tail feathers, the farmer's wife took him to the woods, and tossed him up into the air. He flew away.

'Go and find a wife,' she called, 'and when you have babies, bring them to visit me!' Which is just what he did.

26 January
The magic hat

Two mice want to hide from the cat,
  So they jump into the conjuror's hat.
One whispers low, 'We'll be safe in here!'
  But whose are the footsteps they can hear?
It isn't the cat; it's a man in a cloak.
  The conjuror's seen them! Now for a joke...
He lifts his wand, and taps the hat twice,
  ABRACADABRA! And there in a trice
Are two little rabbits, who scamper away,
  Into the meadow, to play all day.

25 January
The crash

A thin layer of icy snow covered the hillside. Lucy and Arthur decided to pull their toboggan up to the top, and ride down.

'Be careful!' warned their father, 'It may look white enough, but there are a lot of stones showing through; I should wait until some more snow falls if I were you.'

But Arthur and Lucy were impatient; they didn't want to wait. So they puffed up the hill, and then Arthur pushed off from behind while Lucy sat in front.

Faster and faster they went, until a nasty-looking stone seemed to get in their way. The children dug their heels in, to slow down, but it was no good . . . CRASH! A figure dressed in red, and one in green, sailed through the air, and landed with large thuds on the hard ground. How they wished they had waited!

27 January
Chip's adventure

'Don't forget your hat and scarf!' called Chip's mother, as the little sparrow was leaving his nest one cold morning.

Chip flew back, grumbling that he didn't feel cold; but he put them on.

After he had flown all round the wood, saying hello to his friends, he settled down for a sleep on a pile of dry leaves.

When he woke, it had been snowing. He managed to shake the snow off his head, but he couldn't move his wings. Poor Chip!

Luckily his mother found him, cleared the snow off his back, and helped him home. 'How did you find me?' asked Chip.

'I spotted your green hat,' she told him.

28 January
The coincidence

Emily and Anne were expecting their grandparents to come to tea.

'Let's bake some of those delicious chocolate buns that Granny taught us to make, for a surprise,' said Anne.

'That's a good idea,' agreed Emily. Soon the mixture was ready to go into the oven, and the timer was set for twenty minutes.

'We've time to pick some flowers, before Granny and Grandad arrive,' said Emily.

The flowers were arranged, and the buns were cooling when the doorbell rang.

'Look what I've brought you for tea!' said Granny, when she had given the girls a hug. 'Your favourite chocolate buns!'

The girls looked at each other, and burst out laughing! What a coincidence!

29 January
Peto the polar bear

Peto, the little polar bear cub, was playing with his friends the penguins in their playground of ice.

'I can catch fish in the sea, with my paw,' boasted Peto, and showed the penguins how he did it, using his sharp claws.

'We catch fish in our beaks,' said one of his friends, 'not with our flippers.'

'I'm going to catch a big fish, now,' said Peto, and ran off quickly.

'Don't go too far,' warned his friends.

He stopped near the edge of the ice-floe, made a hole, and plunged in his paw. He was so busy with his fishing, he did not hear a CRACK! as the ice he was standing on broke away, leaving him floating away on a small, icy island!

But his friends, the penguins, heard; they all scurried across the ice and plunged into the water to rescue him.

'Hello!' said Peto. 'Seen my big fish?'

30 January
The ballet dancer

Angela was lost in a magic world of whirls and leaps, dancing on tiptoe, or standing on one leg for a graceful arabesque.

In fact, Angela was watching a late performance of the ballet *The Nutcracker* on television. She knew some of the music, and now she was watching the real ballet!

If she half closed her eyes, she could pretend she was there, dancing on the stage, wearing that frilly white tu-tu, then making a deep curtsey to the cheering audience, while someone came to give her a huge bouquet of flowers . . .

'Angela dear, you're nearly asleep!' said her mother. 'It's over, so go to bed.'

How could she explain to her mother that she was pretending to be the ballerina?

Never mind, she thought. Tomorrow she was having her very first ballet lesson, so perhaps she could try again then . . .

31 January
The little donkey

Pepito, the shaggy little donkey, was hot, tired, dusty and bored. Quite early that morning, he had been taken from his stable to the flower market, on the outskirts of the town, and loaded up with big baskets of sweet-smelling lavender bags, and little bottles containing lavender water. Then his master, a boy, had led him into the main square of the town, where they stayed all day, and the boy tried to sell everything he had bought in the morning.

'Lavender!' he called. 'Lovely sweet lavender water! Very cheap – come and buy!'

Pepito's long ears drooped and his head hung down. The smell of the lavender reminded him of the field where he used to live, where the honeysuckle smelled so sweet. Now, the fumes and the noise from the traffic made him feel sick.

At that moment a little girl walking with her mother noticed Pepito.

'Mummy, look!' she called out. 'A sweet little donkey!' She ran over and stroked his nose, and Pepito nuzzled her pocket for something to eat. 'He looks so sad; *please* could we buy him, and take him to live with us in the country? He'd be much happier there.'

Her mother agreed; and soon Pepito and his new little mistress were going for lovely walks in the fields, enjoying the scents and sounds of the countryside.

1 February
Tossing pancakes

Mummy was about to start cooking some pancakes, when Sophie came running in.

'Oh Mummy, please let me cook one! I'm sure I can do it,' she begged.

'Well . . . you can try, but you must be very careful,' said her mother doubtfully.

Sophie was thrilled. Her mother told her when the fat in the pan was hot enough, and she poured a ladleful of mixture in. She waited, and then shook the pan until the pancake was loose.

'Now you can toss it,' said her mother. Up it went, but it stuck to the ceiling! Sophie laughed; and the cat was pleased, as she ate it when it fell on the floor!

2 February
Tibby's busy day

When Tibby had had her early morning run, she decided that this would be a good day to be busy indoors.

Olivia came into the kitchen and gave Tibby some breakfast. After eating her own, she went to school. Tibby watched her go from the window-sill.

While Olivia's mother went shopping, Tibby guarded the house from rats and mice, as she lay quietly on Olivia's bed.

Then came lunch. Oh good! Fresh fish skins; that would give her strength for the afternoon. While the vacuum cleaner roared upstairs, Tibby watched for mice, in front of the fire . . . where Olivia found her, when she returned from school!

'Hello Tibby! Have you had a busy day?' she asked. Tibby stretched, and purred.

3 February
Greedy grey mouse

There was once a grey mouse, living on a farm, who decided to go and see the world.

'I'm catching the train, and going to town,' he told his brothers and sisters, as he packed his best clothes in a suitcase. 'I'm going to see the world.'

He hid in the back of the truck, when the farmer took his produce to the station, early next morning. No-one saw a small grey mouse creep into the goods van in the waiting train. After a minute he smelled cheese, and saw a big round shape near him. In no time he had gnawed through the packing, and was gorging himself on gruyère cheese.

Soon he felt so sick, he wanted to go home! He jumped out of the open door and scurried across the platform, back into the truck, just in time to be driven home.

Poor mouse, he even forgot his suitcase!

4 February
Nature's colours

White is the swan
  With head proud and high.
Pink are the pigs
  Who live in the sty.
Yellow is the chick,
  So fluffy and small.
Brown is the lizard
  Who sits on the wall.
Grey is the squirrel
  Who climbs up the tree
Red is the fox
  Who loves to run free.

5 February
Yellow Bird

Down in the forest Yellow Bird's friends were beginning to feel very worried. They had all overslept, because Yellow Bird had not sung his usual early morning song.

'What's the matter, Yellow Bird?' they called. 'Come and see us.'

Yellow Bird fluttered down to the ground. 'I'm so cold,' he chirped, 'I can't sing.'

The rabbits rubbed him with their warm, soft bodies, until he felt better. They gave him little bits of fur, to line his nest; after that he was always warm at night, and always trilled his dawn song.

6 February
One snowy morning

One snowy morning, the squirrel looked down from a high branch, and this is what he saw: the tomtit, putting on his thick winter tights and woolly cap; the hedgehog, waking up for a short walk, with all his prickles sparkling with frost; and the rabbit, wearing his muffler, and practising walking in his new snow-shoes.

'Hello!' he called, waving a paw to the squirrel. 'Coming for a walk?'

Just then, Peter came along with his sledge, and the rabbit hid. The squirrel decided to stay in the tree, watching.

29

7 February
The fancy-dress party

Robert and William were twins. They looked so alike that many people could not tell them apart – if they forgot that Robert's hair was dark brown, and William's hair was reddish brown.

On their seventh birthday they invited their friends to a fancy-dress party. Robert went as Pierrot, and William went as Harlequin. After the delicious tea they decided to play a trick on the others, so they went to their room and changed costumes! No one noticed, until they took their hats off, and showed their hair.

'We fooled you!' the twins laughed.

8 February
The marmalade kitten

A marmalade kitten
   With stripes on his tail
Went down to the pond
   When the wind blew a gale.
He jumped on a log,
   And the wind was so strong
When he put up his tail,
   It just blew him along!

9 February
The snow fairy

Paul was sitting by the fire looking at his picture book when his eyes strayed to the window. It was snowing, and the snow flakes were drifting on to the window pane, staying there a moment, and then sliding slowly down. They seemed to be getting bigger all the time, and then one took on the shape of a little snowman.

Paul was curious so he put his warmest outdoor clothes and hurried out. He was quickly surrounded by an army of dancing, smiling little snowmen, who pushed him gently along the path.

Soon he found he was floating through the air with his snowy friends, up above the hedges and tree-tops until he landed on a frozen lake in front of an icy palace with tall turrets.

Out of a pointed archway stepped a beautiful lady wearing a long, glittering dress, with silver wings and a shining crown.

'Hello, Paul,' she said. 'I am the snow fairy, and I commanded my snowmen to fetch you, so that I could grant you a wish.'

'Please give the birds something to eat and drink,' said Paul. 'The ground is hard, and the puddles are all frozen.'

The snow fairy smiled. 'Close you eyes,' she said. 'Count three, then open them.'

'One, two, three . . .' Paul was in front of the fire, the sun was shining, and birds were singing outside.

'I must have been dreaming,' he thought.

10 February
Waiting for spring

Becky was watching her father dig a deep, wide hole in the garden.

'What are you going to do, Daddy?'

'I'm going to plant this tree,' explained her father. 'It may look dead, with its leaves all brown, and half of them fallen off, but that's because it's winter. In spring it will grow new leaves.'

'May I plant my flower seeds now, too?' asked Becky hopefully.

'We must wait until spring for that,' said her father. 'When the sun warms the earth, your seeds will grow into flowers.'

11 February
Clumsy Penny

Penelope had been given a doll for her birthday. It was almost as big as Penelope, with fair hair, tied back in a pony tail. She called the doll Penny.

One day Mummy was busy writing a letter, so Penelope took Penny into the kitchen and said, 'We're going to have a tea party!' Soon she had arranged her dolls' tea set round the table, with brown paint water in the tea pot, a bowl of sugar, milk in the jug, and tiny cheese biscuits on a plate.

Then naughty Penny misbehaved! She knocked over her cup of tea, and dropped some biscuits on the floor!

'Look what Penny has done!' said Penelope as her mother walked in.

'She's young; she can't help it,' said her mother, as they cleared up the mess.

12 February
The Nightingales

'Come along, children! It's time for supper,' chirped Mrs Nightingale.

'Oh no! We don't want to come yet,' called the two young Nightingales, who were having a lovely game of hide-and-seek in the branches of the wild cherry tree, where they had their home.

'It's your favourite – stewed worms and beech-nut salad,' said their mother. They flew in and quickly pecked up the food.

'Now, your father and I have decided you are old enough to join us in our evening singing; but you may only sing when we tell you – and one at a time.'

Soon, the warm, sweet trills of the Nightingales' song could be heard all over the woodland. The young birds were very proud to be joining in, too.

Goodnight Nightingales! Sweet dreams!

13 February
Granny's surprise

Robert's Granny loved knitting. Her house wasn't far from Robert's school, and every Wednesday Robert went and had tea with her. After tea his Granny would sit knitting, while Robert looked at books or watched the children's programmes on television.

One Wednesday afternoon, when Granny collected Robert from school, she said to him, 'There's a surprise waiting for you.'

'Is it a toy?' asked Robert.

'No; it's something that's come to live with me. But you can play with it every time you visit me,' said Granny.

When she opened the front door, there was a small kitten, all tangled up in Granny's pink knitting wool!

Robert took the wool off the kitten, and then they played happily together.

33

14 February
Lucky Valentine

There were two very different girls in the same class at school. Mathilda was happy and gay, with lots of friends, while Janet was serious, and shy, and often had no one to play with. They lived in next door houses, in the same street.

When Saint Valentine's day came, some of the children put cards through their friends' letter-boxes, without writing any names on them.

Of course, Mathilda had lots; but one card she should have had was posted in Janet's letter-box by mistake! It showed a picture of Pierrot looking up at smiling Columbine, swinging on the crescent moon. It had a little verse in it, saying:

I wish that you would be my friend,
But I don't dare to say . . .
So if I smile at you, please smile,
And brighten up my day!

Janet was so surprised! To think, there was someone as shy as she was, wanting to make friends!

That day, if someone smiled at her, she smiled back. Soon she had lots of friends.

15 February
Moon Rose

Can you guess which country this little girl comes from?

Her name is Moon Rose, and she lives in a faraway land. She wears a pink kimono patterned with flowers, and shoes with wooden soles. Her long black hair is drawn up into a bun, and held in place with special long hairpins. She lives in a house built mostly of wood, which is lit at night by lights hidden inside coloured paper lanterns. When the weather is hot, she sleeps on a mat on the floor.

Her mother is giving her lessons in flower arrangements, teaching her how to make twigs and small branches look pretty with only a few flowers. There are little dwarf trees growing in the garden, and many brightly coloured birds and flowers.

Moon Rose likes playing with a kite, and she dances gracefully, holding a fan. She knows how to eat her food with chopsticks, and she bows to say 'Thank you'.

Little bells hang at her door, tinkling when a wind blows.

Moon Rose lives in Japan. Did you guess?

17 February
The wild goose

Every year flocks of wild geese flew over Sally's house to escape from the cold weather and spend the winter further south, where the sun is warmer.

One day, while she was playing in the garden, she heard the honk! honk! honk! sound they made as they flew overhead. She looked up and noticed one goose flying behind the others, closer to the ground. It landed in the garden, tired out.

She took it inside, fed it, and looked after it all winter.

In the spring it heard the geese flying back again and flew off with them. Sally was glad; it was back with its friends.

16 February
Old copper kettle

Please sing, copper kettle,
    Oh, sing for us, do!
And tell of the old days
    When you were quite new.
Did the ladies wear hats
    When they went out to tea?
Did they spill on their dresses,
    And make crumbs, like me?
Did they eat bread and honey
    Without any trouble?
Can you tell us, old kettle,
    Or can you just bubble?

18 February
Annabel's doll

Annabel's doll went everywhere with her. Her name was Bella, and Annabel looked after her extremely carefully, which was a good thing, because Bella went in and out of shops, up and down in lifts, and to and fro in cars and buses.

One day Annabel's aunt took her to a big toy shop to choose a dolls' tea set. Of course, Bella had to come too. Annabel put her down for a moment with two other dolls who were having a tea party on the floor, with a plate of five pretend cakes.

When the tea set was chosen and paid for, Annabel went to pick up her doll. She thought Bella had a funny smile on her face, and there were only four cakes left – now wasn't that a strange thing?

19 February
The strange stone

Mark was helping his father with some digging in the garden. They both wore warm clothes as it was a cold day.

Mark's spade turned over something heavy, and he bent down to pick it up.

'Look, Daddy! What a strange stone! It's round, with lines all over it.'

'That's not a stone, you know; it's a tortoise,' said his father, taking it and brushing the earth off its shell. 'He tucked his head and feet in and went to sleep under some earth and leaves last autumn. He's not ready to wake up yet.'

'I'll put him back,' Mark said quickly. He covered the tortoise up, and carefully marked the place with a stick, so he wouldn't be disturbed again.

20 February
My Granny

My son David brought his writing book back from school the other day, and this is what I read in it:

My Granny has a round pink face like a baby's with wrinkles on it. She wears a pair of half glasses which slip down her nose, so she often looks over the top of them.

On Sundays Daddy takes me and my dog Scamp to spend the afternoon with Granny and her dog Rover. Scamp is a small terrier, and Rover is a spaniel. They have a great time chasing each other round the garden, while Granny bakes scones. I love hot scones, with butter and jam.

After tea Granny reads me a story out of her big book. I listen, but Scamp and Rover usually go to sleep.

Granny gets cross if I let earth get on her carpet from my shoes, or make her house untidy. But she is old, and very kind, and I love her.

21 February
The flowers

When Fiona and Clive's mother had done the washing up after lunch one day, they heard her sigh and say, 'Oh dear, I do miss having flowers in the garden! I wish I could go out now, and pick a great big bunch to brighten up the sitting-room!'

Fiona whispered in the corner with Clive, and they both disappeared to their room.

Half an hour later Fiona gave her mother a beautiful flower painting!

'I think Daddy would prefer a car,' said Clive; so that's what he had painted.

22 February
The frozen lake

Claire lived in Canada, where the winter is so cold that the lakes freeze hard, and snow lies on the ground for months.

Ice-skating was Claire's favourite sport, and she was very good at it. She could whizz along quite fast, and then turn and skate backwards, and leap and twirl. There was a lake near her house, and Claire often skated there alone.

'Don't you feel lonely down there, by yourself?' asked her mother.

'Oh no,' said Claire. 'Sometimes the big brown bears keep me company; or if I'm tired, I go for a ride on a reindeer.' She winked at her mother, who smiled back.

23 February
A riddle

I'm big and white and rather fat,
  I wear a scarecrow's battered hat.
My nose is an apple, shiny and red,
  Two pieces of coal are the eyes in my
    head;
I carry a broom and a pipe, for a joke,
  As I do not sweep and I never smoke!
Have you guessed who I am? I'm sure you
    must know,
  If I tell you that I'm only here in the snow.

24 February
The competition

One fine freezing day in the Arctic three polar bear brothers were arguing about who was better at catching fish.

'Have a competition!' said their father. 'See who catches more fish by the time the sun goes down.'

They all caught lots; but as they couldn't count over three, they never knew who won!

26 February
Clever John

John was a clever boy. He was better than most children of his age at reading and writing, and his mother thought his paintings were good – until one day she found him painting a picture of Ruff, the dog, upside down!

'Don't you think Ruff looks odd in your picture?' she asked.

'He looks all right to me,' said John, and painted a picture of a house, with its chimney at the bottom of the page.

While she went to talk to John's father, John grinned turned the pictures the right way up, and pinned them on the wall!

25 February
Bold Billy

Young Billy Weasel was becoming bolder and bolder, wandering further afield each evening in search of food and adventure.

One late afternoon, when he was far from home, he interrupted a family of rabbits while they were out eating their supper, and chased them back into their burrow. The youngest cried for an hour.

'This won't do,' said Mrs Screech Owl to Mrs Brown Owl. 'He'll be after our babies next; let's give him a fright!' So she hid behind a tree near young Billy, and jumped out in front of him, flapping her wings and screeching. Billy turned round and ran away, with Mrs Brown Owl hooting in the air just behind him.

After that, he stayed closer to home.

27 February
The restless star

Once long ago, high in the sky, a star was born. Her name was Stella, and she lived in the Milky Way.

When she was still young – only about three million years old, which is young for a star – she had learned to count up to five, on her points. But she had not learned to keep still. She was always wriggling, and jiggling about, in and out of the other stars, which annoyed them.

Astrologers were amazed as they looked through their telescopes, and saw this small star moving around. Children asked their parents, 'Why is that star jiggling about?' No one knew why.

'When I grow up,' said Stella, 'I'm going to be a shooting star!' So on her 21 millionth birthday, she streaked off to look at the Earth, and the moon, and all the other interesting places in space.

28 February
The Black Forest

Once upon a time, a fairy lived in a big forest, in a country called Germany. She was so shy, she didn't want the sun to see her; so she only came out at night.

But one morning the sun caught sight of her as he rose at dawn. She quickly turned herself into a wild boar, and hid amongst the great trees of the forest, until she could turn back into a fairy at night.

On that day, the lord of a nearby castle went hunting in the forest. He chased a deer past where the fairy was hiding, and the poor little baby fawn was left all alone, shaking with fright, in a thicket.

The fairy was angry. 'Forest,' she commanded, 'turn black! As black as night!'

The forest became so dark that the lord had to stop chasing the deer, and go home.

Ever since then, that forest has been called the Black Forest.

29 February
The new baby

Mummy had been away from home for a week, and Carol was longing to see her again.

Next day, Mummy came home, carrying a baby brother in her arms!

'Oh, can I feed him? And give him his bath? And dress him?' asked Carol.

'You could help,' said Mummy, 'but you'll have to wait until he's a bit older before you can do all those jobs.'

Carol looked disappointed, and Mummy said, 'Here's another surprise!' and gave her a big parcel. Inside was a dressed baby boy doll, with a bottle, in a bath!

'Oh, how lovely!' said Carol. 'Now we can look after our babies together!'

1 March
Chico's army

Chico lived in a hot, dry country called Mexico, where spiky cacti grow, and the people speak Spanish.

One day, Chico's daddy gave him a toy pistol, which went bang when he fired it.

'Hooray!' shouted Chico. 'Watch out, everybody! There's an army coming to capture this village, and I'm the general.'

Then he took his father's big sombrero, and his mother's bright red poncho, and ran down the street to find some friends.

Soon he was marching back at the head of a line of soldiers, all singing: 'We are the army of the re-vo-lu-ti-on!'

Chico ran towards the front door, brandishing his pistol, when his daddy's hat slipped down over his eyes, and he tripped over his mummy's long poncho. Down he fell on the dusty ground. AYEE!!

The general and his army were invited in for orange juice, which cheered them all up.

3 March
Five little pigs

Five little piglets, enjoying a song,
  But as they are singing, who comes along?
It's bad Mr Wolf, and he's hungry today;
  But they are so noisy, they scare him away!

2 March
The rainbow

It was pouring with rain. Jack was sitting in the big armchair, reading, while Joy stared out of the window.

'It says here that at the end of the rainbow there is a pot of gold,' said Tom.

'If I had a pot of gold, I'd buy a pony,' said Joy, 'and a saddle, and a bridle, and a stable to keep him in when it rained.'

'I'd buy a car, and then it wouldn't matter if it rained,' said Jack.

'Look! The rain has stopped, and there *is* a rainbow!' shouted Joy. 'Let's find the gold!' They ran off to look for it.

They crossed two fields, and then the rainbow faded away.

'I don't believe there's a pot of gold at the end of the rainbow,' said Joy. 'I think there are just seven pots of paint.'

When they got home, they each painted a lovely picture – of a pony, and a car!

4 March
Philip's dream

One night, Philip dreamed that a funny little man with a long nose and a tall hat was running about the countryside, doing useful jobs.

'Come on, Flit!' Philip heard him say to the sparrow flying near him. 'Help me sprinkle drops of dew over this field!' It was done in a trice.

'Now we'll start the stream singing,' muttered the little man, 'and next, the flowers must be told to open . . . Oh dear! I almost forgot to visit all the children and give them sweet dreams.'

Philip had never seen anyone dart about so fast.

When Philip told his mother about the little man and his sparrow, she said he was lucky, as no one ever saw him – except, occasionally, in their dreams.

5 March
Who am I?

My trousers are all baggy,
   I wear a funny hat,
My nose is red, my face is white,
   I'm either thin or fat.
I'm always falling over,
   My shoes are far too long,
I'm often soaked with water,
   And things will keep going wrong!
But children love me, everywhere;
   If there's a circus I'll be there!

6 March
The last egg

Mother Hen had hatched out all her eggs but one. The last one was bigger than the others, and paler. Suddenly she heard a quiet *tap! tap! tap!* coming from inside the egg, and out wriggled a baby bird.

But what a surprise for Mother Hen! He looked different from her chicks, with a flat beak and webbed feet.

At first, he played nicely with the others, and did as he was told. But after a few days, he kept wandering off to watch the ducks on the duck pond.

'Come here!' clucked Mother Hen. 'You'll fall in and drown'; but he took no notice.

Next day, he *did* fall in . . . but he swam! 'I'm a duckling, not a chick!' he quacked.

7 March
What am I?

Drink me in the morning,
  I'm tasty and I'm hot,
Drink me with milk or lemon,
  But always warm the pot.
Drink me in the afternoon,
  With toast and cakes and jam,
I'll warm you up and quench your thirst . . .
  Now tell me what I am!

8 March
Mrs Ferret's breakfast

Mrs Ferret woke up one morning feeling very hungry indeed.

'Now what I would really like for my breakfast is two or three fresh eggs,' she thought. Then she remembered having seen a coot's nest on the edge of a nearby lake.

She made her way quickly from the wood where she lived to the reeds at the edge of the lake. Sure enough, there was the nest; but the coot was asleep on her eggs.

'If I'm very quiet, I might have the coot *and* the eggs for breakfast,' thought Mrs Ferret. But she slipped, and fell – SPLASH! into the water.

'Be off, you wicked egg robber!' cried Mrs Coot furiously, seeing who it was.

'Just having my morning bath,' said Mrs Ferret crossly, scrambling out and running home. She had to make do with leftover frogs' legs soup.

49

9 March
The playful rhino

A rhinoceros was passing the time under the hot, African sun, having a dust bath.

Everything seemed calm and peaceful, until a little African boy suddenly appeared, out of breath from running.

'Quick, Rhino, my friend, you must get away from here at once!' he panted. 'A jeep full of hunters has parked over the rise, and one is on his way here!'

'Well, I don't intend to move anywhere else,' said the rhinoceros calmly. 'I'll go and and teach that hunter a lesson.'

The hunter was looking the other way when Rhino tiptoed towards him, and although the men in the jeep waved and blared the horn, it was too late. Down went Rhino's head, and up into the air soared the hunter, to land by the jeep.

'Thank you, my friend,' said Rhino, back in his dust bath. 'I bet they never come here again.' And they didn't.

10 March
White Arrow
and the jaguar

In the vast forests of South America, a young jaguar was waiting for a visit from his Indian friend, White Arrow.

'He's late. What can he be doing?' the jaguar wondered, feeling worried.

He heard sounds in the branches above his head, and looked up. A monkey was coming to give him an urgent message.

'White Arrow has been tied to a tree by his enemy, Black Eagle. You must save him!'

The monkey ran ahead to show him the way, and the jaguar followed. Soon he saw his friend tied to the tree, while Black Eagle danced round it, chanting: '*I will leave you here – till the ants – eat you up!*'

The jaguar sprang on Black Eagle with a mighty roar, pinning him to the ground, while the monkey untied White Arrow.

Black Eagle swore never to harm White Arrow again; so the jaguar let him go.

11 March
Lily's bell

Lily, the lamb, would keep wandering off over the hills, and getting lost. Then Mary, the shepherdess, had to go and find her, and bring her back. It was a nuisance!

One day, Mary decided to tie a bell round Lily's neck. It hung on a red ribbon, tied with a bow.

'What's this for?' Lily asked Shep, the dog. He didn't know. She asked the kittens; they played with it, but they didn't know either. Lily felt puzzled, and sad.

Then the hens and the ducks gathered round her, and said, 'What a pretty sound that thing makes! You do look smart!'

Then Lily was happy. She frolicked in the fields from dawn till dusk, and everyone heard the bell, and knew where she was.

12 March
Fluff and Silky

Fluff, a handsome squirrel, looked out from his home at the top of a tree. He could see everything that was going on from up there, with his sharp eyes.

There was a mole, enlarging his underground house. A dormouse had woken, and was rubbing the sleep out of her eyes. The trees were in bud, and a greenish haze everywhere hinted that spring was on its way.

'I must find some flowers to give to Silky,' thought Fluff. So he ran into a garden on the edge of the woods, and took some flowers from a greenhouse whose windows were open.

Silky was Fluff's lady-love. She was spring-cleaning her home when he arrived.

'Oh, thank you Fluff, they're lovely!' smiled Silky, as she took the flowers. He didn't tell her where he found them!

13 March
Off to the moon

Jenny had just spent a week in bed, with measles. Now she was up and dressed for the first time. But she was getting tired of colouring her pictures.

She left the crayons on the table, and curled up in the armchair. Her eyelids felt heavy as she glanced back at her favourite green crayon. To her surprise, it seemed to be getting bigger, and so did the others!

She heard a small voice, saying, 'Ten, nine, eight . . . jump on, Jenny, if you want a ride . . .' Jenny ran across and sat astride the green crayon, which was now a rocket, '. . . three, two, one, BLAST OFF!' Away she flew, out of the window and up into the sky, rushing straight for the moon! She seemed to be having a race with the other crayon rockets. *WHOOSH!* What fun!

'Come on, Jenny,' said a quiet voice. Was it the man in the moon? No, it was Jenny's father, taking her off to bed!

14 March
The baby donkey

Farmer Bernard loved his animals. He brought them in under cover, when the weather was bad, and he always made sure they had enough to eat and drink. He taught his children, Sophie, Laura and Daniel, always to treat animals carefully too.

One cold night, he thought he heard his donkey braying. So he went out and brought her into the cosy dry stable.

Next morning, Daniel went to visit the donkey. He rushed back, shouting, 'Come and see! Donkey's had a baby!' They all went to look at the baby foal. It was small, with a soft, pale coat, big brown-ringed eyes, long silky ears, and four long wobbly legs.

When he grew bigger, the foal played with the children. His favourite trick was to roll on his back, waving his hoofs.

'Let's call him Roly!' said Daniel.

'Hee! Haw!' laughed Roly; so they did!

15 March
Dressing up

Peter had invited his friend, Kathy, to come and play in the garden, but now it was was raining.

'You could go up into the attic, and dress up in old clothes,' suggested Mummy.

So when Kathy arrived, both the children disappeared upstairs.

Tea was nearly ready, when Mummy heard some strange sounds coming from the stairs; bumping, giggling, and shuffling. Into the kitchen came two odd figures.

'I'm Coco, the clown,' said one, raising a battered bowler hat with one hand, and holding up long, baggy trousers with the other. He had thick red lips and a red nose.

'And I am Madame Mimi,' said the other, curtsying in high-heeled shoes which were much too big, and clutching a huge hat.

They acted their parts all through tea!

'I hope it rains tomorrow,' said Peter.

16 March
Counting rhyme

One – two – three, four, five,
  Once I caught a fish alive.
Six – seven – eight, nine, ten,
  Then I let it go again.
Why did you let it go?
  Because it bit my finger so.
Which finger did it bite?
  This little finger, on the right!

17 March
The odd bird

Mrs Magpie had been sitting on her eggs for days. But when a chick hatched, she was surprised to see that it was brown, instead of black and white.

Just imagine her amazement, when it opened its beak, and called out, 'Cuckoo!'

'How did YOU get here?' she asked the baby bird crossly. Of course, it didn't know that its parents were so lazy they never bothered to build their own nest; the mother bird just waited until it saw a suitable nest, and laid an egg in it, for another mother bird to hatch.

Luckily, Mrs Magpie was kind, so she fed the cuckoo with her own baby birds. Sometimes, they sang this song to him:

A cuckoo is a funny thing,
He only has one song to sing;
What luck for us to have a brother
So QUITE unlike any other!

18 March
Caroline's wish

'It's my turn now,' said Caroline, as she watched her brother on the swing.

Caroline climbed on, and William pushed her to get her going more quickly.

'Higher! I want to go higher,' she called out. 'Oh, I wish I could go as high as the sky!'

A fairy heard her wish, and waved its magic wand. Suddenly, Caroline found herself flying up above the houses and tree-tops. She felt frightened.

'I didn't mean it!' she gasped. 'I wish I could fly down now!' She circled a cloud, and swung down to earth again.

'Was that high enough?' grinned William.

'It's *your* turn now,' said Caroline. But the fairy had gone.

19 March
Patch's day out

Patch was feeling miserable. His master and and mistress had gone to town for the day, and left him all alone.

'Yow-wow-wow!' he howled. He scratched at the door and whimpered, but nobody came.

Two friendly doves spoke softly to him through an open window. 'Come with us!'

Patch jumped out, and followed them to the field. He had a lovely time! He lapped water from the stream, and dug for bones – until a mole asked him not to spoil his house!

'It's time to go home,' cooed the doves, flying overhead. 'Your master is returning.'

Patch got back first. His master patted him, and said, 'Have you been a good dog?'

Patch wagged his tail, and thought, 'I hope he always leaves the window open.'

20 March
Judith's friends

Judith woke up and heard a loud, happy twittering sound coming from outside her window. She ran across the room, and there, lined up on the telegraph wire, were her old friends, the swallows!

'Hello!' she called. 'You must be tired and hungry after your long journey; I'll give you some food.'

Judith dressed quickly, and threw nuts and breadcrumbs to the swallows. She knew they had flown hundreds of miles from warmer countries in the south, where they spent the winter.

'Now I must water the flowers,' she said, looking at the early tulips, and fetching her watering can. A swallow swooped down, and perched on her hand.

'Come and nest at our house, pretty one,' she whispered. The bird flew off, twittering cheerfully.

21 March
Ladybird, ladybird, fly away home

Mrs Ladybird had left her children at home for a while, and gone out in the warm sunshine, to look for food.

She flew slowly round the garden, looking for a flower. Suddenly she caught sight of some tall orange and yellow daisies, so she flew towards them and landed on a yellow one.

'Mmm, how delicious!' she said, tasting the pollen, 'I'm glad the bees didn't get here first and take it all.'

She was so busy eating, that she never noticed the flowers were held tightly in the hand of a little girl, who had picked them to give to her mother.

'Don't go, ladybird!' breathed Jane, as she walked towards the house. But a shadow startled the tiny insect, who flew away.

'I must make sure my children are all right,' she thought, and hurried home.

22 March
Kind Miss Mouse

Mother Robin had gone out, and her four children were making a lot of noise Miss Mouse decided to find out what was going on, so she paid them a visit.

'Oh, dear Miss Mouse what can we give our mother for her birthday tomorrow?' said the oldest. 'We can't decide.'

Miss Mouse thought hard. 'If I brought you some wool which the sheep have rubbed off on the trees, I could help you make it into a shawl,' she suggested shyly.

'Yes! Yes! Bring some quickly!'

Miss Mouse was soon back with a bundle of wool. She showed the birds how to pull it into strands with their beaks, and weave it into a soft warm shawl.

'How did you make it?' asked their mother proudly; but they wouldn't tell.

23 March
Billy's trick

Young Billy Badger was out for a walk, looking for some fun. Most of the animals knew that Billy's idea of fun was often their idea of trouble, so they tried to keep out of his way. But today, old Mr Frog was sitting on a water lily leaf, close to the edge of the pond, dozing, and he didn't know Billy was there.

The naughty young badger crept up very quietly and jerked the leaf up. SPLASH! In fell poor old Mr Frog, while Billy rolled on his back, hooting with laughter.

But the bank of the pond was slippery and sloping, and down rolled Billy with a louder SPLOSH! into the water.

'Serves you right!' croaked Mr Frog, from a leaf in the middle of the pond.

Billy slunk off quickly to dry himself, before anyone asked him why he was wet.

24 March
The fair

I looked out of my window,
    And saw a lovely sight,
A fair had come to visit us,
    With tents of red and white.

The roundabout had started,
    The music sang out loud.
A little man with green balloons
    Was standing in the crowd.

The ices were delicious,
    Strawberry, lemon and lime.
The swingboats swung me up and down;
    I had a marvellous time.

59

25 March
The kind scarecrow

In the middle of a big wheatfield stood a tall scarecrow, on his one wooden leg. He wore an old jacket, which had once been very smart, and a battered hat with holes where the straw stuck through.

Farmer Gruff had put him there saying, 'Now, Scarecrow, you have a job to do here. If any birds come, flap your arms and scare 'em away! D'you understand?'

But the scarecrow loved the birds! He let them perch on him, talking and singing to him, telling him about places he had never visited, and sights he would never see.

One day, Farmer Gruff came to make sure the scarecrow was doing his job properly, but as he approached the field he noticed lots of birds flying away.

'What's going on here?' he shouted. 'If I catch you with any more birds, I'll have you thrown on the bonfire!'

After that, the birds took turns to stand guard. If anyone came, they hid under his coat until the coast was clear!

26 March
Petra's friend

Petra was feeling very excited. She was on on her way home from holiday, and she was longing to see the little foal which had been born before she went away.

When she got off the bus, she ran to the field – but what a surprise! Instead of the tiny, spindly-legged grey foal she had last seen, in the distance was a sturdy young animal!

'Smokey!' she called; but he didn't come. Petra looked in her pocket, but all she could find was a lollypop, which she held out as she walked across the field.

Smokey trotted over and crunched up the lollypop. They were friends again!

27 March
A swallow's nest

All last summer the top half of the old stable door had hung open, only held on with one hinge. No one bothered to mend it because nothing was kept in the stable then, and no one ever went there – except for one swallow, who built its nest inside. and flew freely in and out.

But now, everything was different. Matthew's father had given him a bicycle for his birthday, and as it was kept in the old stable, the door had been mended.

'What's the matter with that swallow?' thought Matthew one day, as one swooped past the stable door, screeching loudly. Then he realized it wanted to use its old nest! So he left the top door open.

After that, Matthew's bike shared its home with the swallow and its family.

28 March
The sand roses

Leila, the Bedouin girl, was very poor. The whole tribe was poor, for it was hard making a living out of the desert, where they lived with their scraggy animals.

'What shall we do, little friend!' said Leila one day, to the desert fox who had become her companion. 'Where can we find treasure, to make our tribe rich?'

The little creature pricked up its ears, and jumped down, out of her arms. It ran across the sand, and Leila followed, wondering where it was going. Soon it stopped, and started digging, until it unearthed a beautiful coral-coloured stone in the shape of a rose. It dug somewhere else and found another . . . and another . . . until Leila took those she could carry back to the camp to show her family.

The sand roses were so beautiful that a sultan bought them, and Leila's tribe had enough money to buy extra food and animals, and have fine tents and clothes.

29 March
Fancy dress

As soon as the grown-ups and the children were asleep, things started to happen.

The dog crept out of his master's room, and told the cat; the cat called to the two ducks outside, who flew up to the attic window; the scarecrow and the tailor's dummy opened the window; and all the others, who had been invited to the fancy-dress party, crept up to the attic to join in the fun.

It was Teddy's birthday party! The dog had managed to scrounge some sandwiches from the kitchen, and dressed as a chef. The ducks played on two old violins while the fieldmouse danced a jig.

'Mmm, very good!' said Teddy, sniffing the food, dressed in a toga.

The owl gave them all a fright, when he flew in at the window saying 'WHOO-HOOO!' with a sheet over him, pretending to be a ghost. And the cat looked *very* elegant.

I wonder what time they all got to bed!

30 March
The blue feather

Down from the sky one day came twisting, whirling and drifting, a blue feather. It landed in a little girl's hair, but didn't stay there long.

Soon a breeze lifted the pretty feather and dropped it on to grandmother's lap. *Atchoo!* She sneezed, and sent the feather wafting down on to the cat's paws, as it lay deeply asleep. The feather moved gently with the cat's rhythmic breathing, while the dog watched it . . .

Up and away again went the lively blue feather, caught by another invisible gust, while the dog leaped up and snapped at it, missed it, and woke the cat.

This time a swallow caught sight of it; thinking it was a butterfly, the graceful bird turned, dipped and *snap!* had it in its beak. Disappointed, it let the feather go . . . down, down, down it went again, falling into my open book.

So I kept the feather; here it is!

31 March
Lazy Long Ears

Long Ears, the young hare, didn't feel like going to school. The sun shone warmly on the fresh meadow grass outside his home and he wanted to be out there, practising his somersaults and cartwheels.

'All your friends have to go to school,' his father pointed out. 'Why not you?'

Long Ears couldn't think of a good answer, so he set off, unwillingly, along the woodland path that led to his school.

Just imagine his delight, when he met some of his classmates running towards him, shouting, 'No school today! Miss Owl has lost her voice!'

'Hooray!' shouted Long Ears. 'Let's play ducks and drakes on the pond!' The ducks scattered when Long Ears and his rowdy friends arrived, and started sending small flat stones skimming over the water.

'Caw! Don't wake the fox!' warned a crow. Long Ears ran off. When he was hungry, he asked a hen to share her lunch.

'Not until you've done some work,' she said; so he painted some of her eggs.

'I'll be an artist when I'm big,' he said.

1 April
April Fool!

On the 1st of April Nancy noticed her mischievous brother writing something on a piece of paper, and sneaking quietly out of the front door. She followed, and saw him pinning the paper on the back of old Mr Thompson's coat, without his noticing. It said I'M AN APRIL FOOL!

Nancy felt sorry for the old man, as all the children were giggling and pointing at him. So she managed to take the note off his coat, and fix it on her brother's, without his noticing!

He didn't find out until lunch-time!

2 April
Good old Caesar!

Janet and John had just returned from the fields with Caesar, the big farm horse. They unhitched him from the cart, and gave him a carrot to munch, as a reward.

Suddenly, Caesar pricked his ears and whinnied loudly. The children looked across the fields, and saw a tall tent standing on the village green, and some white horses being led into it.

'The circus! The circus has come!' they shouted, and Caesar neighed again.

'Let's take him to see the horses,' said Janet. 'He deserves a treat.' So they both clambered up on to his broad back, and clip-clopped off down the lane.

When they reached the big tent, the last white horse was going in. Caesar followed, and before they knew it, he was cantering round the ring, while they hung on! Everyone clapped and cheered; it was the best act they'd ever seen!

4 April
The new baby!

The neighbours were puzzled. They knew there were four children in the family next door – two boys, who often kicked their ball over the fence, and two younger girls, who liked playing with their dolls – so who, or what, was in the pram?

The youngest girl was pushing the pram gently round the garden, while the other danced alongside, saying 'It's my turn now! Let me push him now.'

Perhaps they had a baby brother – or a new doll. The neighbours didn't like to stare, because staring was rude, but they wanted to know what was in that pram.

Suddenly, a little furry creature wriggled out and jumped on to the lawn.

It was a kitten! Did you guess?

3 April
Hoppity's friends

Hoppity Frog lived all alone in the reeds at the edge of the pond. He was young, and liked playing in the water, but there was no one for him to play with, and he was too timid to leave the pond and look for a friend.

'Someone is coming!' whispered the pink butterfly one day. Down to the pond came Mrs Duck with her four ducklings, to give them their first swimming lesson.

'Hello!' croaked Hoppity politely. The ducklings all crowded round him in surprise; they had never seen a frog before, and admired his smart green skin and long legs.

'Can *you* swim?' one duckling asked. Into the water dived Hoppity; and soon they were all swimming and playing together.

6 April
Bunny rabbit

Bunny rabbit in your hutch,
  Fluffy fur, so soft to touch,
Nibbling lettuce all day long;
  Will that keep your sharp teeth strong?
Big bright eyes look out and say,
  'May I please come out and play?'
Now the door is open wide,
  So run, and hop, and jump outside!

5 April
A ladybird's job

A pretty little ladybird was spending the afternoon on a rose bush, sunning herself and trying in her rather slow, gentle way, to chase away the greenfly who would try to eat the leaves.

A busy, buzzy bee flew right inside a beautiful pink rose near the ladybird. When he flew out again, she asked him, 'Do you chase away the greenfly too?'

'Certainly not, you silly thing!' buzzed the bee rudely. 'I have a much more important job to do. I collect nectar to make into honey.'

The poor little ladybird felt ashamed and she crept under a leaf to hide.

The rose spoke softly to her. 'You are very important to us, dear ladybird. If you didn't try to keep the greenfly away, they would eat the leaves and the buds, and there would be no flowers; and no nectar for the bees!'

The ladybird crawled out, happy again.

7 April
Snowball's sweet tooth

Snowball was a small white kitten. But although she looked very sweet and charming, she was, in fact, extremely naughty and disobedient – not about everything, but about food, in particular. Her mother had told all the kittens that sweets and chocolates and sugary things were bad for their teeth, and the others were sensible and didn't eat them – well, not often.

But Snowball took no notice of her mother's advice. She took sweets when no one was looking, and ate them behind the curtain. The silly kitten used to forget to throw away the papers, so she was always found out, and spanked.

But it made no difference; if there were no sweets, she went to the cake shop, and the lady there would give her some unsuitable, sweet, sticky cake.

One night, Snowball woke up with bad toothache. Her mother comforted her as well as she could, and next day took her to the dentist – a big dog called Mr Ivor.

'There's a hole in your tooth,' growled Mr Ivor. 'Have you been eating sweets?'

Snowball nodded miserably.

'It'll have to go,' barked Mr Ivor, and pulled it out.

Snowball wanted to keep her other teeth, so after that, she ate the right food.

8 April
Friendly slow-worm

I am called a slow-worm,
  Don't confuse me with a snake!
If you ever find me,
  Please don't make that sad mistake.
I would never harm you.
  'Though I'm quick, and very shy,
Pick me up and hold me,
  Touch my skin; it's smooth and dry.
Always friends with gardeners,
  Eating insects, snails and slugs.
They would spoil your vegetables;
  No one wants those nasty bugs!

9 April
Billy the kid

Down in the stable, on a comfortable bed of straw, a baby goat was born. His mother, the nanny goat, licked him carefully all over. Soon he started bleating in a thin, high little voice which Sam heard from outside. He ran quickly into the stable, and was just in time to see the kid having his first breakfast of warm milk.

'I shall call you Billy, the kid!' said Sam. 'Now try and be good.'

Billy the kid was soon strong enough to walk. When his mother took him out in the field for the first time, he sniffed the fresh grass, looked up at the great blue sky, and started running and jumping for joy! The nanny goat watched her son for a while, and then she browsed sleepily on some thistles, happy that all was well.

A pretty blue butterfly flew over Billy's head, searching for flowers. It fluttered away, towards the path edged with wild roses and cowslips. Billy was curious, and followed it down to the stream.

The nanny goat looked up from eating and couldn't see her son. 'Maaa! Maaa!' she bleated anxiously.

'Maa! Maa!' came an answering bleat from Billy, so she trotted off to find him.

Sam had to fetch them from the stream! After that, he firmly fastened the gate.

10 April
What can you see?

How many puppies are looking at a tree?
How many rabbits are eating their tea?
How many kittens are doing a dance?
How many snails are out, taking a chance?
Five young . . . what are these,
　　Running on the grass?
Here are six . . . something else,
　　Letting time pass.
Seven fluffy swimmers,
　　An eighth on the edge.
Nine woolly . . . who are these,
　　That scrambled through a hedge?
How many are black,
　　And how many white?
And how many swallows
　　Are resting from their flight?

11 April
Richard's garden

Richard liked trying to do things to help in the garden. But the trouble was that whenever he found something that looked interesting to do, somebody stopped him.

His father took a rest from painting the gutters under the garage roof; so Richard climbed up to see if he could do some painting, but his father called out, 'Hey! Come down! It's dangerous up there.' So he looked for something else.

His grandfather had been cutting wood for the fire, and had left the saw out.

'Poor grandfather! He's old, and someone should help him,' thought Richard. So he picked up the saw and tried to move the sharp, jagged blade across the wood; but it kept jumping sideways.

'Better put that down, old chap,' said grandfather, hearing the noise from his garden chair. 'You might get a nasty cut.'

Richard went sadly inside to look for his mother. 'Whatever I do in the garden is wrong,' he told her miserably.

'Cheer up! I have something which I was saving for your birthday next week, but I think you should have it now.'

She gave him a brown paper parcel. In it were a small-sized spade, fork and rake, and packets of flower and vegetable seeds.

Now Richard could make his own garden!

12 April
Lucky flowers!

Although Jed was only two years old, he knew quite a lot about the garden. He knew the names of several birds and flowers – and when he didn't know about something, he usually made up an answer.

Jed's favourite bird was the robin, and he had made up his mind that when it flew round the garden, singing its busy song, it was telling the flowers to grow!

One day, Jed was very worried as he couldn't see the robin anywhere. 'The flowers won't grow,' he thought sadly.

He took his harmonica into the garden, and played tunes to all the flowers.

They didn't stop growing; and luckily the robin returned – with a wife!

13 April
The rescue

Brenda Bunny lived with her parents and her brothers and sisters in a burrow on the the safe side of the stream. It was safe because the rabbits knew everyone who lived there. There was a dark wood on the other side, full of secrets.

Brenda Bunny was very curious. One day, she persuaded Mrs Duck to give her a lift across the stream, on her back. She hopped into the wood. In a minute she was running for her life from a fox! SPLASH! She escaped into the river – but she didn't know how to swim.

Luckily, Mrs Duck managed to rescue Brenda, who promised not to stray again.

14 April
The baby fairy

There was great excitement in Fairyland. A beautiful new baby had been born, and as was often the custom when the baby fairy was a girl, she was going to be named after several flowers, who were asked to be her godmothers.

Many flowers and fairies had been invited to the christening. A grand feast was being prepared, of nuts, and fruit, and honey or rose-hip jelly.

The baby lay in a rose-bud, sleeping, while the godmothers brought their gifts.

'I bring you beauty,' said the rose.

'I bring purity,' said the lily.

'I give my colour to your eyes,' said the forget-me-not, 'and my faithfulness.'

'And I bring sweetness,' said the honeysuckle, touching the fairy's cheek.

So Rose Lily Forget-me-not Honeysuckle woke, smiled, and the party began.

15 April
Little green dragon

Sally and Ian were walking by the stream one sunny morning when all of a sudden something green scurried across a rock right in front of them.

'Ian, look!' cried Sally 'A green dragon!'

Ian tutted impatiently and put on his long-suffering face – why did little sisters have to be so soppy?

'It was a lizard and now you've scared him away . . . Anyway, there's no such thing as dragons, silly!'

'There is too!' said Sally indignantly. 'I've got a picture of one in my book, only mine looked much too big to fit on that rock. Perhaps it was a baby dragon?'

'Sshh . . . keep very still and he might come back,' whispered Ian.

Just then the little lizard crept out again to bask in the sun.

16 April
Forgetful Kanga

Young Kanga, was always arranging to play with a friend, but he had a very bad memory.

One day, he arranged to meet a friend and wondered how he would remember.

'I know!' he thought. 'I'll tie a knot in my tail, and then I *can't* forget!'

But when the time came, poor Kanga just could not remember *who* he was supposed to be playing with. So he bounded off, hoping he might bump into the right friend.

'Am I supposed to be playing with you?' he asked Koko, the koala bear, hopefully.

'No,' replied Koko, 'but seeing that knot in your tail reminds me that I must fetch something for my mother,' and he ran off.

'Hee! Hee! You do look funny with that knot!' squawked Pip, the parrot. Kanga decided to go home, and untie the knot.

Plato, the platypus, was waiting for him. 'Don't you want to play with me?' he asked.

'Oh yes, Plato,' said Kanga. 'I shall always arrange to meet friends at home; then, if I forget, I'll just wait here!'

73

17 April
Anna learns a lesson

Anna had been given an adorable white kitten with blue eyes and little pink pads, and a beautiful doll, with chestnut brown hair and green eyes.

But Anna could not, or would not look after her two new friends properly.

She teased the kitten, dangling a plaything above his head, but never letting him have it. Then she held his front paws, and made him dance all over the house on his hind legs. The kitten bit her hand, and Anna threw him unkindly outside.

As for the doll – she often left her on the floor, half dressed, and never bothered to put her to bed at night.

'I shall have to teach Anna a lesson,' decided her mother one evening, and she left the kitten and the doll with Granny.

Next morning, when Anna's mother told her that her two friends had run away to find a kinder mistress, she cried and cried, and said if they came back she would take great care of them, and always be kind. After two days, they *did* come back! And Anna kept her promise.

19 April
The timid chick

Five tiny fluffy chickens were born one day – four were yellow, and one was speckled brown.

Mother Hen was soon bustling about, chivvying them into a good corner of the yard to find seeds and grubs to eat.

'Now, copy me,' she ordered. 'First you have to scratch at the ground with one foot, while you stand on the other; whoops! Mind your balance! 'Speckles had fallen. Next moment he was running away!

'What's the matter?' clucked his mother.

'A green monster is coming to eat me up!' peeped Speckles, very frightened.

'Come back!' said his mother. 'It's a caterpillar, and *you* should eat *it* up!'

18 April
Gone fishing

Michael and Jennifer were as happy as could be! A stream ran past the end of their garden, with weeping willows lining the banks, and tied firmly on to one of the willows was a boat. It was big enough for them to sit in with fishing lines and a basket containing a picnic lunch or tea. They spent hours in the boat every day, always joined to the bank by the rope.

One day, the knot in the rope came undone, and the children drifted away!

'Hooray! Let's go round the world!' shouted Michael bravely.

'How do we get back?' wailed Jennifer.

Luckily, their father heard them, and ran along the stream with a boat-hook. He waded out and pulled them in.

After that, they checked the rope every day to make sure it was safely tied.

20 April
Impatient Colin

Colin was an impatient boy. Whenever anything nice was planned for the future, he always wanted it straight away.

If he was given sandwiches and a piece of cake for tea, he ate the cake first.

As for waiting for things like Christmas and birthdays – that was hardest of all!

'Daddy, what are you giving me for my birthday?' Colin asked one day.

'Wait and see!' said his father. But Colin could not wait; he wanted to see now.

He thought the spare room was the most likely place to hide a present – and he was right! In a cupboard he found a parcel with FOR COLIN written on it. He opened it, and found a big kite inside.

He ran close to the sea, and managed to get the kite up in the air, but . . . the wind tugged it away, and it fell in the sea.

Poor Colin! He had to tell his father.

21 April
The reward

It was raining, and the four kittens could not play outside. Poor Mother Cat was being driven nearly mad, because they got under her feet while she was working, and made all the rooms untidy. She decided to give them something special to do.

'Who wants a reward?' she asked.

'I do,' said Greycoat quickly.

'What's a reward?' asked Snowflake.

'A reward is something really nice. Whichever of you makes the nicest birthday present for Aunt Lily, will get a reward. You have two days to make it!'

The kittens thought it was an exciting idea, and set about deciding what to make.

Greycoat took some clay and made a vase, decorating it with paw prints.

Ginger made a careful drawing of a bunch of flowers, and then chose lots of lovely colours to paint them.

Brownie took some of his precious modelling clay, and made a model of a cat.

Poor Snowflake couldn't think what to make. Then she had a good idea.

'I'll write a beautiful poem,' she decided.

On Aunt Lily's birthday, they all went round to her house with their presents, and a cake which Mother Cat had made.

'Oh, thank you all very much!' she said.

'Who gets the reward?' whispered Ginger.

'You all deserve a reward, so I'm taking you out for a picnic!' said kind Aunt Lily.

23 April
A rain storm

Pitter, patter, pitter, patter,
　That's the raindrops' favourite song.
And for snails it doesn't matter,
　They hope it rains all day long!

Trickle, trickle, the rain mutters,
　'Gainst the steamy window panes,
Flowing down the roofs and gutters,
　Filling all the outside drains.

In the house the firelight's gleaming,
　Susan and her doll are warm.
Cat and dog are sleeping, dreaming,
　They don't care about the storm.

22 April
A strange dream

Paul was playing in the garden, while his mother sat knitting in a deck-chair.

Paul could smell the lovely scents of the spring flowers. He began to feel dizzy, and then so light that his feet left the ground, and he started to fly! He looked over his shoulder, and saw that he had two delicate blue wings – he was a butterfly!

He fluttered over to his mother, and brushed against her cheek.

'Oh! What a beautiful butterfly,' she exclaimed. 'If only I could catch it and show it to Paul.' But he flew off and landed on the ground. When he tried to fly again, his wings had gone!

'Mummy, I had such a strange dream,' he said; but a flower shook its head at him.

'Maybe it really happened,' he thought.

24 April
Happy birthday

Michael and Mandy were twins. A few days before their fifth birthday their mother said they could send out invitations to a few friends for their birthday tea party.

The twins wrote the names on the cards and Mummy addressed the envelopes.

'Take some money, and buy a box of crackers at the corner shop,' said Mummy. 'You can post the invitations on the way.'

On their birthday, the twins helped to decorate the table with pretty plates and mugs, and crackers. Mummy had made them a big cake with ten candles on it (five for each twin), and all they were waiting for was their friends, with some presents!

'They are late,' said Mummy. 'Did you post the invitations?' Mandy gasped and burst into tears. They were in her pocket!

'Never mind; come and see my present,' said Mummy. Waiting in the neighbour's house was a dear little puppy, asleep.

'We'll have one party now, and another with your friends next week!' she said.

25 April
Primroses

Jackie lived with her mother and father on the edge of a big forest.

One fine spring day, Mummy said, 'I wish I had a big bowl of primroses in the sitting-room! But there are only a few in the garden, and I like to see them growing there when I go out.'

'We could buy some from the market,' said Jackie, but Mummy shook her head.

'The flowers you buy are never as fresh as those you pick yourself,' she said.

'It's the warmest day we've had this year; coming for a walk in the forest, Jackie?' said Daddy suddenly. She agreed, and they set off together.

The trees were bursting into leaf, and everything was fresh and gleaming.

'Daddy, look! Hundreds of primroses! How lucky you brought a basket!' Jackie's father smiled, and they started picking.

26 April
Eleanor's trunk

Eleanor Elephant had a bathe with her parents in the river every day. As she was still young, her mother helped her wash; but she decided one day it was time Eleanor learnt to do it on her own.

'You must learn to use your trunk,' she said. Eleanor dipped the end of her trunk in the water and blew hard. Of course, all she did was blow bubbles!

'No, no, silly child!' said her father crossly. 'You have to *suck* first.'

Eleanor breathed in deeply, with her trunk under water. She coughed and spluttered, and a little green frog shot out of her trunk and landed on her mother's head.

'Never mind,' said her mother. 'All you need is practice! Now, go and have your tea. I've left some of your favourite ripe water-melons on the bank over there.'

While Eleanor was in the middle of eating the melons, a huge, fierce tiger sprang out of the bushes at her, roaring loudly. Eleanor got such a fright that she choked. The seeds from the water-melon went the wrong way up her trunk, and she sneezed violently, shooting them out with great force, hitting the tiger between the eyes. He fled into the jungle, terrified.

Eleanor's parents *were* proud of her!

28 April
The race

One day, Boris, the wild boar, managed to get right into the middle of a field of maize. He was really enjoying himself crashing about, biting off and chewing the tasty green shoots, when a squeaky little voice interrupted his thoughts.

'Look out, you clumsy elephant!'

'Who dares to speak to me like that?' snorted Boris furiously.

'I'm Fred, the fieldmouse. You should look where you're going; you nearly trod on my tail!'

'Get out of my way!' shouted Boris.

'I'm not afraid of you,' squeaked Fred. 'What's more, I bet I could race you to that oak tree!' Away sped Boris, not aware that Fred had jumped on his back! When they reached the oak tree, Fred sprang lightly down over Boris's nose, in front of him! After that, Boris always hung his head when he walked – as do all wild boars.

27 April
Greg's garden

Greg had been asking his father if he could grow some seeds, and now he had dug over a corner of good earth, shaded from the mid-day sun by some lilac bushes.

Greg smoothed the surface with a small rake, planted his seeds carefully, at intervals, watered them with his own watering can, and then waited for something to happen.

Next day, Greg saw a slight movement in the earth. 'One of my seeds is growing!' he shouted. Then he saw a worm wriggling out of the ground. Greg was so cross, he threw the worm as far as he could.

When his father explained that worms air the ground and help the roots to grow, Greg spent ten minutes looking for the worm. But he never found it!

29 April
Young detectives

'Gosh! I'm bored . . .' yawned Bill, the three-month-old basset hound.

'Me too,' grunted his brother, Bob, stretching lazily. 'How about going down to the wood to play hide-and-seek with your friend, Hoppity Rabbit?'

'Good idea,' replied Bill, and led the way at once towards Hoppity's burrow. But when they arrived, they saw a group of Hoppity's friends, looking worried.

'Hoppity's vanished! We can't find him anywhere,' said the little red squirrel.

'We must organize search parties,' said Bill Basset. 'Squirrels, you could look all around the trees; deer, you search along the paths; and birds, you fly up over the trees, and let us know if you spot anything unusual. My brother and I, having very good noses, will sniff around and try to pick up scent clues.'

By nightfall, no one had found out anything, so Bill and Bob went sadly home.

Curled up, asleep in their kennel, they found . . . Hoppity! He'd come to visit them!

30 April
The letter-box

We have a letter-box nailed to the gatepost at the end of our drive, to save the postman a walk.

Last spring, I ran down to collect the letters one Monday morning. Instead of letters, I found some bits of moss.

'That's a funny thing for the postman to leave,' I thought.

On Tuesday, a bird's nest was inside! So I left a note saying PLEASE USE TIN, and put a biscuit tin beside the gate-post.

On Wednesday – two little eggs.

On Thursday – two more eggs!

On Friday, when I peeped in, two bright eyes and a sharp beak were pointing at me.

On Saturday, I stuck up a notice saying OCCUPIED!! DO NOT DISTURB!

On Sunday, I nailed up a new letter-box!

2 May
The butterfly

Mark had a colouring book with a large picture of a caterpillar in it. His mother told him that if he looked carefully in the garden, he might be lucky and find one.

He did find one and brought it inside on a leaf to show his mother. Together, they found a large empty glass jar, jabbed plenty of air holes in the lid, and put several leafy twigs from the same bush inside, with the caterpillar.

After some time, Mark said, 'It has wrapped itself up in a white blanket!'

After still more time, out crawled . . . a lovely butterfly, which flew away.

1 May
Lucky lilies!

Every 1st of May, when the dew is on the grass and most children are still sleeping, Belinda and Dido, her donkey, walk into the woods, where the lilies-of-the-valley grow.

'Mm . . . don't they smell lovely?' thinks Belinda, picking herself a bunch. When the two baskets on Dido's back are full, they walk together to the town, and stand at a street corner, to sell the flowers.

'Lilies! Fresh lilies! Bring you luck the whole year through!' calls Belinda.

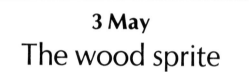

3 May
The wood sprite

Tiny wood sprite, in the tree,
  Why do you like teasing me?

When I searched deep in the wood
  Where lilies-of-the-valley should
Be growing thick, I heard you say,
  'I've hidden all flowers away!'
Not one lily could I find.
  Wood sprite – why be so unkind?

Off to the wood again I went,
  Taking a basket, for I meant
To pick wild strawberries, and share
  Them with my friends; but he was there,
That naughty sprite! I heard him hoot,
  'Ho! Ho! I've eaten all the fruit!'

I knew that something *must* be done,
  And so I planted, one by one,
Some good, strong strawberries, in a row,
  And lilies; there I watched them grow.

Now, tiny sprite, be friends with me!
  I'll give you flowers, and fruit for tea!

5 May
Pretty ladybird

'Pretty spotted ladybird,
    Crawling round all day;
What do flowers say to you,
    To while their time away?'
'They tell me their secrets,
    That they cannot tell you . . .
Why wood anemones are white,
    And cornflowers are blue.'
'Pretty spotted ladybird,
    Do you know how to fly?'
She watched a swallow, spread her wings,
    And flew up in the sky . . .

4 May
The golden spider

Zelda, the golden-coloured spider, lived
all alone, up in the loft. She wove her web
across the skylight, and often longed to be
out in the fresh air and sunshine.

So one morning she crept down the loft
ladder, scuttled across the landing and
down the stairs, and *swish!* a broom swept
her into a pile of dust. She shook the dust
off, and carried on towards the open door,
when *pounce!* the cat just missed her. She
hid under a low chest until it was safe to
run outside.

'Whew! That's better,' thought Zelda,
breathing in the fresh air. Suddenly, *peck!*
A bird's beak snapped, as she jumped
sideways to avoid it. With her eight legs all
shaking with fright, she rested under a rose
bush, and then climbed up it.

'You'll be safe here,' whispered the rose,
'but don't talk to the lizard!'

Zelda wove a web close to her friend.

6 May
The warm island

Coral Flower lived on an island where the sun shone nearly all the time. She had thick, long black hair, and wore a flower-patterned dress called a sarong.

The island was very beautiful, full of pretty flowers, trees and birds. The sea was so clear you could see coral growing a long way under the surface.

Coral Flower's father went out in his boat early every morning to fish. Coral Flower liked to watch for his return, while she played happily for hours on the beach. From there she could see the smoking mountain, called a volcano.

One morning Coral Flower heard the volcano rumbling. It shot flames up into the air, and she could feel the earth trembling. A stream of hot lava poured down the distant mountain-side into the sea, making it rough.

Coral Flower rushed home, frightened, thinking of her father. But he had landed at another beach, and was already back!

7 May
Moonlight

Do you know which creatures like to come out at night, when the moon is shining? Let's open the window, watch and listen . . .

Whoo-hoo-hoo! That's the owl, up in the woods. *Rustle, rustle* . . . who's this coming now? It's mother hedgehog, snuffling around with her two children! *Tri-li-li!* Can you hear the nightingale's sweet song?

Some say, when the moon is full, the mist fairy changes from a deer into her fairy form. Can you see her out there?

8 May
Rosebud's day

Rosebud wakens in the morning,
    Stretches crinkled petals, yawning,
Sips the night-time's gift of dew,
    Wonders what he's going to do.
Now the sun is high, and strong.
    Little rabbit comes along,
Stops to have a quiet rest;
    When you're hot, the shade is best!
Rosebud feels a nasty tickle . . .
    Something's trying to eat his petal!
Luckily, a bird flies by
    And makes a meal of one greenfly.
Afternoon brings drowsy heat,
    Bees collect the nectar sweet.
Evening comes; and cool at last,
    Rosebud's glad his day is past.
Soon he'll be a full-blown rose;
    Will he be picked? Nobody knows.

9 May
Beginner's luck

'I've got a very special present for you, Daniel!' said his grandmother one day. 'I'll give you a clue: what is very long, and light?'

'A very long balloon?' suggested Daniel.

'No! Better than that,' smiled Granny. 'Come with me to the shed, and we'll see if you can find it.' Daniel was very excited, and ran ahead. When they were in the shed, she helped him by saying, 'You're cold . . . warmer . . . getting warmer . . . there! You've got it.'

'It's Grandpa's old fishing rod!' Daniel was thrilled with his present, and hugged Granny with delight.

'Your Uncle Hugh can take you down to the river now, and show you how to use it.'

Soon uncle and nephew were sitting side by side on the river bank. In ten minutes, Daniel had caught a trout!

'Beginner's luck!' laughed Uncle Hugh.

'It's the rod that's lucky,' said Daniel.

10 May
Coloured balloons

My new balloons have blown away,
   So I shall search for them all day.
First, I asked the hedge and trees:
   'Did a green balloon pass, please?'
'Yes, one did pass overhead,
   But it didn't stop,' they said.
I asked the apples on the tree
   To catch my red balloon for me.
An apple lying on the ground
   Said, 'You can eat me when it's found!'
And when I asked the corn to look,
   It said, 'One's floating in the brook!'
A prickly rose said, 'I did see
   A pink balloon fly far from me.'
'And where's my favourite blue balloon?'
   'Up in the sky!' replied the moon.
All my balloons have gone away,
   So I must buy some more today.

11 May
Rose, the Sleeping Beauty

I'm sure you know the story of the Sleeping Beauty, who slept for a hundred years. This story is rather like it: but it happens every year.

Once upon time, a beautiful pink rose was held as a prisoner by nature. She was closely bound in a tight green covering, with only a tiny tip of pink showing.

Many bold princes tried to help her to escape: Jack Frost threw hailstones at her prison doors, but they didn't move.

The sun shone in springtime, and managed to open the doors a little; but nature would not let her out. A warm breeze blew gently through the gap, but still the rose had to stay inside.

Then the young prince of early summer came, and set her free! For this was the time that nature wanted her to come out, in all her beauty. How happy she looked, smiling and waving at all her flower friends in the garden.

12 May
The kind clown

Della had been Susan's favourite doll for a long time, but now she had been left at the end of the bed, all alone. 'Susan doesn't love me any more,' she thought.

You see, Susan had just had a birthday, and she had been given a clown doll with a funny red nose and clown's costume. Now she played with him all the time.

Susan had gone to sleep with the clown doll in her arms, instead of Della.

After a while, the little clown heard Della crying. He was a kind little chap, so he quietly went and wiped her eyes, and lay down beside her, holding her hand. 'I'll be your friend,' he said.

Susan found them together next morning. 'I must play with you both, now!' she said.

13 May
Happy birthday!

Why do the butterflies
　Flutter round your head?
Why has a sparrow come?
　What is it he said?
Why has a wood pigeon
　Landed on your shoulder?
Has someone told them all
　You're a whole year older?
Why do the ladybirds
　Make bracelets on your arms?
Why do the flowers nod?
　Are they envious of your charms?
Why are two turtle doves
　Perching on your dress?
They've all come on your birthday,
　To wish you happiness!

14 May
Helpful Caroline

'Caroline! Lunch is on the table,' called her mother. 'Hurry up! It's getting cold.'

'I think she's in the garden,' said her father. He went outside and called her name; but no one came.

A startled blackbird flew out of a tree, giving his alarm call. Then their big black cat ran by, coming from the same direction.

Caroline's father looked towards the tree and noticed some leaves shaking.

'Is that you, Caroline?' he called.

'Hush, Daddy!' came her urgent whisper. 'The baby blackbirds are learning to fly!'

'And you are helping them, are you?' Her father was used to her funny ideas.

'Of course I am,' replied Caroline. 'Can't you see? I'm keeping the cat away!'

15 May
The fawn

One evening, when the sun had set and the sky was already dark, a pretty young fawn was playing in the woods.

Suddenly, he stood quite still, gazing up in amazement as something brilliant hurtled through the sky. He ran to his mother, and said, 'Someone's just thrown a star across the sky, Mummy!'

'No one threw it,' said the mother deer. 'That was a shooting star.'

'I'd like to be a shooting star,' said the fawn, skipping with excitement.

'Do you want to leave me?' asked the doe.

'Oh no, Mummy!' The fawn forgot the star.

16 May
A Chinese tale

In the Valley of the Rising Sun, the people were all very worried. A great deal of rain had fallen and filled the river so full it had overflowed its banks, and ruined their rice harvest. The people were afraid they would all go hungry.

One night, a little girl called Light of Dawn had a very strange dream.

Next morning, she did what the dream told her: she wrote a letter addressed to a prince who lived a great distance away, in a palace on the banks of the same river, telling him about their troubles. She painted one of her pet fish gold, tied the rolled up letter to it, and placed it in the river.

A fisherman found the golden fish, and gave it to the prince as a present. He read the letter, and sent rice to the hungry people. Light of Dawn was so grateful, she sent another gold painted fish to the prince; and that is how the first goldfish was born!

17 May
Rosemary

Rosemary lived with her parents in a pretty cottage on the edge of the forest.

The little girl loved woodland flowers. As it was her mother's birthday the next day, she decided to go into the forest and pick her a beautiful bouquet.

After lunch, Rosemary set off with a basket, and was soon enjoying herself looking for her favourites. But she didn't notice how far she had wandered into the forest, or how dark it was getting. The moon appeared, making strange shadows fall across her path. She sat down and cried.

Then a friendly owl hooted nearby. Rosemary decided to follow the sound, and the owl led her all the way home!

She left the flowers in a bucket of water, as a surprise for the morning, and ran indoors to find food for the kind owl.

18 May
The little prince's animals

Ali, the little Indian prince, had been ill. Although he was much better, he had to rest every afternoon. He preferred to be outside on a couch, in the shade of a tree, where he could watch his animals.

'I'm the most beautiful creature here,' squawked the parrot, showing off her beautiful colours.

'Well, I'm the biggest,' said the elephant, 'so I must be the best!'

'And I'm the cleverest!' said the monkey. 'Which of us is the best, Ali?'

'I prefer Fido, my faithful dog,' said Ali. 'He always stays quietly by my side, and never boasts, or shows off.'

19 May
Frisky's friend

Today was a sunny day – just the sort of day I like – so as soon as Frisky popped out of his hole (by the way, Frisky is a fieldmouse), I joined him.

I never bother to ask Frisky if I can keep him company, because he always seems quite happy when I'm there. He never talks to me, and I don't talk to him. But we do everything together! When he jumps, I jump; when he eats, I eat too; if he runs, there I am, running beside him, or behind him, or sometimes in front of him.

This afternoon it rained, so I left him, because I don't like rain. Can you guess who I am? I'm Frisky's shadow!

20 May
The naughty twins

Two beautiful little twin lambs were born in the meadow, early one morning. They were snowy white, and looked so alike that their mother hardly knew them apart.

When they grew older, they started to get up to all sorts of tricks!

One would take the poor hen's eggs, and hide them; then the other would chase the ducklings down to the pond, or pull the old sheepdog's tail while he was asleep.

Their mother would get very cross, but if she scolded one, he would blame his brother, so she never knew which was the culprit.

The turkey, whom the lambs never dared to tease, came to the mother sheep, and said that *something had to be done* about those two scamps. So she made one wear a blue ribbon, and the other a red ribbon; Then everyone knew who did what, and when!

21 May
Igor's pipe

Igor was a goat-herd. Every morning, early, he took his father's herd of goats from their house in the valley up into the higher pastures. He used to whistle merrily, all through the day, and the goats seemed to like the sound, for they always followed him and never strayed.

One day, Igor's father gave him a pipe, to play his tunes on. But when he tried to play it, he couldn't make the notes sound right, and the goats ran off! So Igor took some music lessons from his father, and after that the goats never strayed again.

22 May
The garden fairy

The garden fairy was asleep on her bed of lilac, with her head resting on a soft pillow of sweet-scented pinks. At dawn, when the birds woke her, she pushed aside her coverlet of petals and stepped gracefully out of bed.

First, a quick bath in the dew collected in a peony. Then, breakfast of nectar, sucked from the petals of clover flowers.

'Now I must write my invitations for the summer ball, and send them to all my friends,' she said. Sitting on a king-cup stool, she wrote a friend's name on each flower invitation, using a dove's quill as a pen.

'Wood sprite . . . tree elf . . . rainbow fairy . . . toadstool goblin . . .' she murmured. 'Oh! I mustn't forget the moonlight fairy!'

The goldfinch delivered the invitations one by one, while the other garden birds started to make her a magnificent ball gown of flower petals, embroidered with crystal dew drops. When evening came, the garden fairy was the belle of the ball!

23 May
Lonely harlequin

Every day, Jimmy liked to go and play in the woods. He loved climbing trees, and swinging on branches, rather like the lively red squirrel who came and played near him. He brought titbits to feed the wild animals who became his friends.

One day, Jimmy's grandmother gave him a harlequin suit, made from different coloured pieces of material, all sewn together. He put it on, and asked if he could go and show it to his friend, Bill.

'Yes, of course you can,' said his mother. 'But mind you keep it clean!'

Jimmy ran through the woods, keeping to the path. The squirrel pelted him with pine cones, and his two rabbit friends took one look at him and bolted.

'Oh dear!' thought Jimmy, stopping. 'I don't feel like me in these clothes!' He ran home, changed into his old jeans, and went to play with his woodland friends.

24 May
Making jam

The fruit is in the saucepan,
  Now get the sugar out!
Weigh it, pour it in,
  And stir it all about.
When the mixture's bubbled
  For just the time it should,
Pour it into jam pots!
  Mm, it does taste good!

25 May
The magic mirror

Miriam's bedroom window looked across the street at another window, just like hers. She often noticed an old lady with white hair sitting alone in that room, looking sad. Miriam watched her stroke her cat and talk to it, and she thought the lady looked kind.

One day a flower seller came down the street selling bunches of violets. Miriam took some pocket money and bought some violets for the old lady.

'I've seen you, too!' smiled the lady, when she thanked Miriam. 'And now it's my turn to give you a present.' She fetched a round mirror in a black ebony frame.

When Miriam hung the mirror on the wall of her bedroom, it showed the whole room, including the floor and the ceiling!

'That's because it curves outwards,' explained her mother. But Miriam preferred to think it was magic, she saw the old lady in it, waving to her, and waved back.

26 May
The diamond bird

Tamara lived high up in a block of flats. The people who lived in the flats were not allowed to keep dogs or cats. This was disappointing for Tamara, as she loved pets, and longed to have one of her own.

One day, when Daddy came home, he put a large package on the table, and called her.

'You have been working so hard at your reading,' he said, 'I have decided to give you a special present.' Tamara took the paper off as fast as she could, and there was a beautiful green birdcage! And inside was an even more beautiful bird.

'It's called a diamond, and comes from a very distant country,' explained Daddy.

'Oh, thank you, I love him!' said Tamara. 'Look at all his bright colours: red head, black scarf, purple waistcoat, yellow tummy and green wings. He's the handsomest bird I've ever seen! But won't he get lonely, by himself in there?'

Tamara's Daddy smiled. 'Every time you do some really good work, I'll give you a diamond.' Tamara looked at the cage, and imagined it full of all the pretty birds she wanted to win.

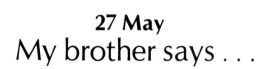

27 May
My brother says . . .

My brother says
   He's not afraid of bears.
And, if he saw one,
   He'd push it down the stairs.
There's only one
   That he'll see in this house.
And that's his teddy bear
   Who'd never hurt a mouse.
My brother says
   That ı pushed him downstairs.
I say it was a bear
   Who caught him unawares!

28 May
Counting rhyme

One, two
   Flowers for you;
Three, four,
   I'll pick some more.
Five, six,
   Up to my tricks!
Seven, eight
   Sorry! Can't wait . . .
Nine, ten,
   Eating again!

29 May
The woodpecker

Robert was feeling very excited. He lived with his family in a big city, and he had been invited to spend a whole week in the country with his grandmother. He had never been away from his mother before for longer than a weekend.

'Good-bye, Mummy!' he called, feeling a little lonely as she drove away, leaving him at Granny's house.

Suddenly, he caught sight of a brightly coloured bird on the branch of a pine tree. 'Look, Granny! Is that a parrot?'

'No, he's a woodpecker. But he certainly is bright, with his yellow body, green wings and gay red cap! Tomorrow, if you like, we can take a picnic into the woods. We shall hear him tapping away with his sharp beak on the wood, and looking for insects to eat.'

Robert was thrilled! What a lot of things he would have to tell his family!

30 May
Flying high

I wish I were a butterfly,
  With pretty coloured wings
Of yellow, purple, pink and blue;
  I'd see so many things!
I'd flutter round the birds and bees,
  And visit all the flowers;
I'd come and go just when I pleased,
  And fly around for hours.
But butterflies cannot fly high . . .
  I'll take an air balloon,
And throw out all the sandbags
  Till I reach my friend, the moon!

31 May
Losing teeth

When one of my teeth comes out, do you know what I do? First, I wash it carefully. Then I put it inside a small cardboard box, under my pillow for the night.

When I look next morning, there's always a silver coin in the box, instead of my tooth. Mummy says the fairies take it; but why should they want to buy my teeth? I wish I knew . . .

1 June
Brave Stephen!

Stephen always felt rather nervous about going into the woods alone, perhaps because he had read too many stories about wolves living in faraway forests. So, when his mother asked him to take a basket into the woods and pick wild strawberries, he went; but he sang a song to keep his spirits up:

Who's afraid of the big bad wolf?
Big bad wolf! Big bad wolf!

Suddenly, Stephen heard a rustling sound coming from behind some bushes. Using all his courage, he went to have a look. He was amazed to see a squirrel, holding up its paw, obviously in pain.

Stephen picked up the poor frightened creature and put it in the basket. 'Did you think I was the big bad wolf?' said Stephen, smiling at his own fear.

He took it home, bathed and bandaged its paw, and kept it until it was better. Then they were friends, and after Stephen set it free, it often came back to visit him, or played with him in the woods.

2 June
Ferdie's friends

Ferdie looked just like his fox cub brothers, but he didn't behave like them. When they wanted to play pretend fighting games, he wanted to play hide-and-seek. When they wanted to play stalk-and-pounce, he wanted to play hunt-the-hazel-nut-shell (which mother vixen used as a thimble).

He wandered sadly down to the river, and met some ducklings. He let them hold his tail with their beaks while he swam, and gave them rides on his back. Then he played leap-frog with two young squirrels.

'Come back tomorrow!' his friends called as he ran home. What a happy day!

3 June
The elves' picnic

Each summer, when the leaves and grass of the woodland are still a fresh, light green, the elves hold their moonlight picnic. The chief elf decides each year which night to hold it. He wakes in the early morning, sniffs the air, listens to the birds singing, looks carefully at the sky, licks his finger and holds it up to check for wind, and measures how fast the plants are growing.

If all the signs are right, he sends his elf messengers out to blow a special fanfare on their flower trumpets, telling all the elves that the picnic is tonight!

They dance and tell stories and eat and drink from dusk till dawn; so, if you find an elf asleep next day, don't wake him!

4 June
A frog

Something strange has happened to me.
  I feel different; what's this I see?
Webbed toes, where my feet should've been,
  And I've shrunk! My skin has gone green!
Croak! Croak! Did you hear what I said?
  If this is a dream, I'll wake up in bed.
I'm cold squatting on this damp lily leaf.
  Oh, Mummy! I'm me again; what a relief!

5 June
The lost ball

One day Laura lost her ball in the woods. She put it down while she went to pick flowers and forgot where she had left it.

'What's this?' said a puzzled squirrel. 'Is it alive?' He sniffed it nervously.

'Maybe it's something to eat,' said his friend, the grey rabbit. He licked it, and pulled a face. 'Yuk! It tastes nasty,' he said, backing away from it.

'It's a ball, that children play with,' chirped a bird, who flew everywhere and saw many things. 'Laura left it behind.'

'Shall we play with it?' suggested the rabbit, patting it gently with his paw.

'It's too big; I'd rather play with oak-apples. Let's roll it to the path, so Laura will find it,' said the squirrel.

Next day, Laura was amazed to find her ball so easily!

6 June
The two friends

A cheeky, bold little shrimp made friends with a rather timid small fish. They played together in the shallow rockpools that formed when the tide went out; but they were not allowed to go out into the deep water.

'There are big, dangerous fish living out there, who would eat you up in one second,' warned the small fish's mother.

One day, when the two friends were chasing each other round in the shallows, the bold shrimp said, 'I'm bored here; the last one to reach that island is a coward!' And off he darted.

The timid fish didn't want to be called a coward, so he followed his friend, planning to pass him at the last moment.

But a fierce shark, waiting in the deep water, saw the shrimp and ate him up. The timid fish swam quickly back home.

'I'm glad I'm a coward,' he thought.

7 June
The grateful elf

Sue and Dinah ask one day,
　'May we go down the lane and play?'
'Yes,' says Mummy, 'here's some food.
　Bring some flowers, and please be good!'
In the lane they find an elf
　Feeling sorry for himself.
He's so tired, he shares their tea,
　For there's plenty there for three.
'You have been so kind to me,
　Close your eyes! Count three!' says he.
When they look, the elf's not there,
　But lovely flowers grow everywhere!

8 June
The big baby

Oliver often helped his grandfather in the garden at weekends. He had his own wheelbarrow, which he pushed all over the garden. Sometimes he loaded it with garden rubbish; sometimes he put small tools in it; and sometimes he pushed it along quite empty, noticing things.

'Look, Grandad!' said Oliver, in the garden one Saturday. 'There's a funny fat bird with no tail, sitting on a log.'

'Sh! Stand still, and you'll see something interesting,' whispered Grandad. 'It's a baby cuckoo, learning to fly.'

'I can't see the mother cuckoo,' said Oliver. Just then a bluetit flew down to it with a juicy worm.

'Cuckoos lay eggs in other birds' nests,' explained Grandad; 'Now the bluetit's the cuckoo's mother – although she's smaller!'

Oliver tried to imagine his mother being smaller than himself. What an odd thought!

9 June
The dragonfly

Dragonfly,
   Flutter by,
In your dress of tulle!
   Darting flight,
Quick as light,
   By the blue-green pool.
Hovering,
   Shimmering,
Hanging now in space.
   Just your wings,
Fragile things,
   Move at lightning pace.

10 June
The greedy pair

'Woof! Woof! Hooray! Here comes our dinner,' barked Barney and Bob, as Frances brought their midday meal out on to the grass, in one large, red bowl. The two little spaniel puppies were such messy eaters that she usually fed them outside, where she wouldn't have to clean up.

Barney jumped up and knocked the bowl with his paw, spilling some food, even before they had started eating!

'Naughty dog!' scolded Frances; but Barney didn't look at all sorry. He just wanted to get more of the dinner than Bob.

After their meal, both puppies' long ears were messy, and had to be washed.

Then Frances thought hard, and had an idea. Off she went to the pet shop with some money, and came back with two parcels . . . one smaller bowl for each dog! Their ears wouldn't get in the food so easily, and they couldn't eat more than their share!

12 June
Bright Feather

Bright Feather was a little Indian boy. One day, he decided to visit his friend Little Bison, who lived downstream with another tribe, by the same river.

'Come on, Lucky!' he called to his pet monkey. 'And Squawker, you're coming too!'

They all sat in the canoe. Squawker, the parrot, looked out for rocks, Bright Feather paddled, and Lucky waved to friends on the bank!

When they arrived, Bright Feather pulled the canoe up the bank, made his special call to Little Bison, and soon had a fire lit. They would want to cook fish later, and the smoke would keep mosquitoes away.

Little Bison arrived with a tent. That night they feasted on fresh fish, and next day Bright Feather returned to his tribe.

11 June
Biff and Buff

Biff and Buff were two naughty little bear cubs. Although they didn't mean to, they were always getting into trouble.

One warm afternoon mother bear was fishing for salmon on the banks of a quiet pool, fed by a rushing stream, while the bear cubs played together and rolled about on the grass.

'Sit still a minute,' said Biff. 'I think I can smell honey!' Now honey was their favourite treat, and they only had it on special occasions.

They sniffed the scent, and followed it to a hole in the trunk of an old oak tree. They both had their snouts in the hole, trying to lick the honey, when some bees returned and couldn't get in! They were so angry, they stung the two robbers!

The cubs couldn't sit down for a week!

13 June
Floppit's picnic

Angela's best friend was her pet grey rabbit, Floppit. She had been carefully training him to behave well when she let him out on the grass for runs. Now she only had to call his name and he came to her at once. She always gave him something to nibble when he came.

'We're going for a picnic today, Floppit,' said Angela. She set off, with Floppit hopping happily beside her, until they reached a pretty spot by a stream.

Angela spread a cloth on the grass, and put the food on it, including lettuce and radishes for Floppit.

'After lunch, we could paddle, or pick flowers,' said Angela. But when they had eaten, she felt so full, and tired from the walk, she dozed off to sleep!

When she woke, Floppit was asleep!

'Good little rabbit!' said Angela. 'I'll bring you here again another day!'

14 June
Hungry hedgehog

One evening, at dusk, just as the first pale star appeared, a hedgehog came out of his home in the woods, and decided to visit a vegetable garden belonging to a house nearby.

'I'll be all right, so long as that great big four-legged hairy monster doesn't run out of the house, and frighten me away with that loud noise he makes,' muttered the hedgehog. 'I never run out and snort at him, when he runs through my woods; why should he do it to me?'

The hedgehog squeezed through the hedge, and soon found a tasty slug to eat. Then . . . 'Woof! Woof!' The big dog from the house bounded up, barking loudly.

'Come here, Pip!' said a man sternly. 'That hedgehog is our friend, because he eats the pests that nibble our plants.'

The dog went away, the hedgehog uncurled itself, and went on eating.

15 June
Tit for tat

Tom was on the beach, close to the water, when the tide was going out. Suddenly, he noticed the damp sand quiver and shake.

'What's that?' he wondered, and dug with his spade. Out came a surprised crab.

'Oo! I'm taking you home in my bucket,' said Tom, delighted with his find. He tried to pick the crab up, but it pinched him hard. 'Horrid creature!' he yelled.

'Well, you were horrid to disturb me!' said the crab, scuttling into the sea.

16 June
Ian goes fishing

Ian was allowed to fish in the shallow stream that ran past the end of the garden. He set off one morning with his fishing line, basket and bait, sure he was going to catch lots of fish.

'There'll be one for your dinner, Puss,' he promised, as his cat strolled some of the way with him, sniffing the bait.

Ian sat on the bank for a whole hour, and didn't get one bite. The cat joined him, and watched. Then it saw a fish in the stream close to the bank. It leant over, and scooped with its paw in the water. SPLASH! It fell in.

Ian put down his line and jumped into the water to save the cat. But Puss swam bravely back to the bank alone, while Ian waded back, his trousers soaked.

In the stream the fish bubbled with laughter, and the two fishermen went home.

17 June
The stowaways

Linda was feeling so happy, she couldn't stop jumping for joy! Her mother had just told her that they were all leaving the next day to spend their summer holidays at Grandfather's farm. Linda loved going there, mostly because of all the animals, which she helped to feed and look after.

'I shall see the dappled horse with the wavy mane, and the gentle cows, and the funny pink pigs with their curly tails, the donkey, the hens and chicks . . . and all my other friends on the farm!' said Linda.

'We're going by train, so please don't bring any toys; they'll be too heavy,' said Mummy. Linda looked sorrowfully at Jemima Doll and Teddy.

'You'll have to stay behind,' she said.

That night, her two friends crept very quietly into her suitcase, and hid.

They wanted to see all the animals too!

18 June
The starfish

Topsy was a very pretty little starfish. Her mother was proud of her daughter's sandy pink colour, and her five beautiful arms, and tried to protect her.

'Stay close to me, Topsy,' she would say as the little starfish swam off to play with the sea anemones on the rocks. 'Someone will see you, and pick you up, and take you away to dry and keep as an ornament. That's what happened to your Aunt Betsy!' But Topsy took no notice.

One warm afternoon, Topsy went close to the shore to play with some young crabs. A boy was paddling nearby, looking for shrimps, and caught Topsy in his net! He was so excited to see the starfish that he dropped the net by mistake, and Topsy swam out just in time.

She hurried back to her mother, and promised to be more sensible in future.

19 June
Lucky Smokey

Smokey, the grey pony, gave rides to children on the beach. His favourite rider was a little boy called Philip, who rode well and didn't pull his mouth too hard.

One day Smokey found himself being taken in a van to a field. He was saddled and bridled, and told to wait.

'I wish I knew who was going to ride me,' he said nervously, to a friendly rabbit.

'There's a kind boy who lives here; I expect he'll ride you,' said the rabbit.

Smokey looked up, and saw Philip coming!

20 June
The bee's song

I'm a busy honey bee,
  Working all day long,
Taking nectar from the flowers,
  I sing my buzzing song.

Please don't disturb me while I work!
  I'll sting you if you do.
There's honey in the hive to make,
  Enough for me – and you!

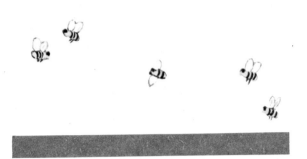

21 June
Billy know-all

Billy, the farmer's boy, thought he knew how to do everything. One day he saw the farm cart standing in the yard, loaded with vegetables for market. Twig, the pony, was waiting to be harnessed to the cart.

'I can do that,' thought Billy. He fastened the leather straps, jumped into the cart, and called 'Gee up!'

Twig set off down the lane at a fast trot. Unfortunately, Billy didn't know how to manage the long reins. So when Twig saw some fresh grass in the field, and swerved through an open gate to reach it, Billy couldn't stop him.

The harness came undone, Twig trotted off, a cart wheel caught on a rock, and the vegetables spilled on to the ground.

Billy ran away and hid, all day!

22 June
The swallows

'Mummy! Mummy! The swallows are back!' Diana could hear their shrill cries, and saw them circling and swooping outside the house. 'Look! They're rebuilding their old nest under the window.'

Diana ran up to the dark, dusty attic, and stood quite still beside the one small window. She could see the birds at work, dipping low over the stream, and flying to the old nest with dried grass. and mud, which they cleverly wove in.

Her cat, always curious, followed her to the window, trying to look out.

'From now on, Sam, you're not allowed in here; you'll frighten the birds,' said Diana, putting him outside.

Soon five eggs appeared in the nest. Then the mother kept them warm, while the father fed her. At last five baby birds were hatched, fed, and taught to fly.

Wasn't Diana lucky to watch it all?

23 June
A fairy story

Once upon a time a little bluebird was hatched out of a tiny blue egg. He looked ordinary enough, but he always seemed to be hungry, so the mother and father took turns to fly off and fetch food for their fledgling.

The trouble was that as well as having a big appetite, he was also very fussy about what he ate. He only liked eating blue things, such as cornflower petals, bluebells, and blueberries.

When he learned to fly, he could search for food himself, but he never seemed to find enough to eat.

One day a fairy felt so sorry for him, that she decided to make a magic spell.

DING! She waved her hand in the air, and turned lots of grey mushrooms pale blue! The bluebird had plenty to eat.

So, if you ever find blue mushrooms growing, be sure to leave them alone. A hungry bluebird will probably eat them.

24 June
Laurence's bell

Laurence, the lamb, had been given a red bell to wear round his neck. He jumped and skipped in the field, very proud of the pretty tinkling noise he made.

The young fieldmice danced along the path to school, when they heard the bell, and a butterfly flew down to admire it.

The birds chirped all the louder, and the other lambs were very envious.

'I shouldn't go near the owl with that,' warned the squirrel. 'He's asleep.' But Laurence ran right under his tree.

'Go home! *Whoo-hoo!*' hooted the owl loudly, and flapped his wings in Laurence's face.

Poor Laurence ran home, and stayed there!

25 June
Sleepy Starlight

Starlight was one of the fairies of the night whose job was to protect the gentle animals that come out to feed at dusk.

One evening, when the sun had set but there was still enough light left to see, a little grey rabbit came out of its burrow to feed. Just then Starlight woke, stretched, and watched the little creature hopping about and nibbling the grass.

A weasel came out of the woods to look for its dinner, and saw the rabbit. 'Ah!' she thought, 'Here's a tasty morsel!' and licked her sharp, greedy chops.

At the same moment a dog ran into the glade, and spotted the weasel. He began to chase the weasel, who began to chase the rabbit, who ran for shelter near the night fairy. She was so confused that she waved her wand by mistake, and turned them all into toadstools – naughty Starlight!

26 June
Summer heat

In summer heat,
  I like to eat
Out on the grass,
  And let time pass
Me slowly by . . .

A swan floats there
  Without a care
Upon the stream;
  I lie and dream
Under the sky . . .

The fish won't bite
  Until the light
Begins to fade,
  And welcome shade
Brings out a few . . .

An evening breeze
  Begins to tease
The wilting flowers,
  Who pass the hours
Longing for dew . . .

27 June
Three pink pigs

Three little pink pigs lived with their mother, the sow, in a field not far from the sea. One hot summer's day they all decided to play on the beach.

'Take your sun hats,' said the sow; but they didn't take them.

They had a lovely time paddling in the sea and making sand castles; but their poor pink little faces got very sunburnt and sore.

'You look like three tomatoes!' laughed a seagull. The piglets found some flour in the barn which they sprinkled over their heads, before they dared go home again!

28 June
Balouka's trip

Balouka, the bear cub, led a very happy life in the forest. All day long he played with his friends, climbed trees, ate wild honey, fruit and sweet berries. He also liked to watch the boats chugging past on the river which ran through the forest.

One day he jumped in the river and swam away to see where the boats went.

When he reached a port, he climbed ashore. Everyone ran away from him! He walked into a shop, and the people all screamed! Balouka didn't understand why.

The shopkeeper locked him inside the shop window, and for a while it was fun waving at the people who laughed at him.

But when a man came with a chain, and opened the window, Balouka ran past him, and didn't stop until he got home!

30 June
Sophie's dream

Sophie felt sleepy, and a little bit bored in the garden today. She lay on a rug under an apple tree, watching a butterfly.

'Come on!' The butterfly was talking to her! 'You'll be late for the party!'

Sophie jumped up, and followed the butterfly behind the tree. The party had already begun; some ladybirds were dancing a jig, while a grasshopper played his fiddle. Ants were running everywhere, serving refreshments. A choir of bees droned a song in close harmony.

'Now it's your turn,' they told Sophie. 'Oh dear!' she said, and woke – on the rug!

29 June
What are honey mice?

Once upon a time, in Australia, there lived a pretty little mouse. Usually she was the happiest of creatures; but one day a kind bee heard her sobbing her eyes out, all alone.

'Whatever is the matter?' buzzed the bee, flying down beside her.

'I'm tired of being a mouse; I want to make honey and fly, like you,' gulped the sad little creature.

Now, this bee had the power to grant a wish every evening, and so far on that day she had not granted a wish.

'You can make honey,' said the bee, 'but I cannot give you wings as well.'

'Oh thank you, thank you! Kind bee!' squeaked the mouse, happy again.

That is how the honey mice came to be in Australia, where they have lived happily ever since.

1 July
The page boy

Arthur, the little page boy, lived at the top of a tall tower in a castle many years ago. They didn't have schools then, so Arthur had lessons at home, in reading, writing, sums, history, music and dancing.

Arthur had just learnt a new song, and the singing master was pleased because he had sung it well. It was a song about a battle, fought many years ago:
Father, what is that distant beat?
  It sounds like drums, and marching feet.
Yes, my son, they have gone to fight
  With swords and shields, a splendid sight.
Father, what is that bugle call?
  There's victory in its rise and fall.
Hurrah! The battle's over, son,
  Our foes are beaten; we have won!

'Can I go and play now?' asked Arthur hopefully. He was tired of having lessons.

'Yes, you can go now; but you must be back in an hour for your dancing lesson.'

Arthur ran down the two hundred and ten steps from his room into the garden.

'Why do I have to work, while you do nothing but buzz?' he asked a bee.

'I work all the time, taking pollen to the hive; I can't go and play, like you,' buzzed the bee crossly.

Arthur stood and thought; perhaps he didn't have such a hard life, after all.

2 July
The lazy weasels

Poor Mrs Weasel was in despair about her two young weasels. Although they were getting quite big, they were too lazy to search for their own food. They would return home in the late afternoon, after running round the woods, visiting their friends, and having a gay, carefree time, and say hungrily, 'Well, Mum, what have you brought for our dinner tonight?'

Mrs Weasel had to spend most of her day finding enough food to satisfy her lazy, greedy daughters, and it made her tired.

One evening, she decided she had had enough. 'As from tomorrow,' she said, 'you can hunt for your own food.'

When they returned the following afternoon, they both looked full and happy.

'What did you find?' asked their mother.

'Oh, a bit of this and that,' said one.

'We ate enough,' said the other, vaguely.

Mrs Weasel followed them next day, and found the lazy pair tucking in to a meal prepared by kind Mrs Hedgehog!

3 July
Peace and quiet

Every fine Sunday in summer, Granny and Grandpa invited their two noisy young grandsons to spend the day with them in the country. The boys' parents came too, and chatted with Granny and Grandpa while the boys played cowboys and Indians.

About four o'clock Grandpa would yawn, say 'Just off for a spot of fishing,' and disappear for three hours. The boys wondered why he never caught any fish.

One day they crept down to the river, and saw him asleep in his fishing chair.

'He just comes for a bit of peace and quiet!' they guessed, and left him alone.

4 July
Kind Katy

Katy was a very tender-hearted little girl. She had been watching over a beautiful red rose in the garden, to see that it came to no harm, when one day she saw some holes in its leaves. She found a caterpillar, but didn't like to give it to the birds. So she threw it in the bushes, thus saving the rose and the caterpillar.

5 July
My fish

My name is George and I am six years old. I am going to tell you about fish.

There are three kinds of fish. Some live in the sea, where they know all about big waves, and what ships and sailing boats look like from underneath. Fishermen try to catch them in big nets, and with rods and lines from boats, or from the shore.

Other fish live in rivers and lakes, where the water is not salty. Fishermen try to catch them, too, with rods and lines.

The third kind of fish lives in a glass tank, called an aquarium, or in a glass bowl – like my goldfish. I feed him on special fish food which I buy from the pet shop. There are plants growing in the sand, and he enjoys himself swimming round and blowing bubbles. Fishermen never try to catch this kind of fish.

6 July
On the beach

Keith was seven years old before he had the chance to spend a holiday by the sea. They lived on a farm near mountains, and either his father was too busy in the summer, working on the farm, or they took a short holiday in the mountains.

But now Keith and his mother were to spend ten days with cousins at the seaside, and Keith wanted to spend every minute of every day on the beach!

He ran down to the water, and put a toe in. It was colder than he expected! A wave rolled in, and he ran back quickly; it went back, and he followed it. He turned to look at his mother, and SPLASH! a big wave caught him, and wet him all over!

Next, he tried to make sand castles with buckets of dry sand – but of course, they crumbled straight away.

'I'll look for shells,' he thought, and spent the next hour making a lovely collection, which he gave to his mother.

'Oh thank you, Keith,' she said. 'There is a lot to learn about the beach, isn't there?' Keith nodded. He didn't mind.

7 July
Breakfast time!

'Who's that, tapping on the pane?'
   Tap! Tap! Tap! 'It's there again.'
'Lazy Jane, get up and see!
   Sammy Sparrow's here – that's me!'

'Quick! Get dressed, or you'll be late;
   Leave some breadcrumbs on your plate
For I'm feeling very hungry, too.
   Chirp! Chirp! Chirp! I'll sing for you.'

This is Sammy's lucky day,
   For now that breakfast's cleared away,
There are lots of crumbs to eat,
   And bacon rinds. Mmm! What a treat!

8 July
The circus clown

Nicholas was so excited! The circus had come to town, and since early that morning the circus people had been busy putting up the Big Top and preparing for the evening performance. Nicholas gazed through the railings, fascinated.

Once, a funny little man from the circus smiled at him, and said 'Coming tonight?' Nicholas nodded, and the man said, 'I'll look out for you!'

When the time came, Nicholas had a ring-side seat! First came the beautiful white circus horses, with red plumes nodding on their heads, as they trotted and cantered round the ring with the music. When the ring-master cracked his whip, the horses danced on their hind legs.

Next came an amazing juggler, who tossed skittles, plates and balls up in the air, never dropping one! After him came the acrobats, who did their daring act high up, swinging across above the crowd, and balancing on the tightrope.

Then came everyone's funny favourite – the little clown! With his baggy trousers, long shoes, and painted face, he soon had the children roaring with laughter.

Suddenly, he recognized Nicholas, and threw him his hat! Nicholas *was* proud.

9 July
The enchanted mill

An old watermill had stood empty for years. It was in a beautiful part of the forest, built on the banks of a clear stream, and many wild animals lived nearby. Unfortunately for the animals, many people came from the towns to picnic there, leaving behind their litter, sharp tins and bottles.

The forest fairy, who protected animals from danger, felt sorry for them, and cast a magic spell round the old mill and its garden. A thorn hedge sprang up, through which only animals could find a path.

After that, it became an animals' paradise! Deer ran freely in the garden; rabbits tunnelled under the thick stone walls of the mill to make their burrows; raccoons splashed merrily in the stream, and squirrels spent happy hours leaping from the roof on to the turning mill wheel, and on to the ground, while birds flew by.

As far as I know, it is the same today!

10 July
The shy ostrich

In the old days ostriches were thought to bury their heads in the sand when they were frightened, or didn't know what to do; this is a story about an ostrich who missed a chance by burying her head!

One day a pretty young lady ostrich was going for a stroll, stepping out on her long, shapely legs, when a young rhinoceros caught sight of her. He was very impressed by her elegance.

'Dear Miss Ostrich,' he said, in his rough, booming voice, 'Will you marry me? You are so beautiful, and I can protect you from all harm!' He lumbered across on heavy, thick legs, nodding his head in what was meant to be a friendly way; but Miss Ostrich was embarrassed by his words and frightened by his horn – so she quickly buried her head in the sand!

Rhino was rather short-sighted, and when he looked at her, he said, 'No head? I can't marry someone with no head!'

He turned, and galloped off very fast!

11 July
Good neighbours

One fine sunny morning Mrs Fieldmouse decided to go shopping.

'Now, my little ones,' she said to her family. 'Stay inside until I come home.'

She set off with her basket, with a cheery word for everyone she passed.

'Hello, donkey!' she called. 'Is your sore hoof better? Good morning, Mrs Hen, and how many chicks have you now?' and so on, all the way to the shops and back.

But what a dreadful shock awaited her! Her nest had been ploughed up!

'Hee-haw! Here are your babies,' called the donkey, from the next field. He had seen the plough coming, and rescued them by putting his head down, and letting them scamper up his face and sit between his ears, holding on to his mane!

12 July
The legend of the dragonfly

Once, long ago, before there were any dragonflies, a magic dragon lived in a cave beside a quiet lake. The trouble was that it was too quiet for the dragon, and he was very lonely. A fairy felt sorry for him, and visited him every day.

But once, when she knelt by the lake to scoop up a handful of water to drink, she slipped and fell in – without her magic wand in her hand to save her!

She didn't know how to swim, and shouted for help as loudly as she could.

The dragon heard her from the other side of the lake; having no time to run round and save her, he blew with his magic hot fiery breath on to the lake, turning all the water into steam, and the fairy into a misty-winged, sparkling insect.

People called this insect a dragonfly – perhaps because of this strange legend.

13 July
The sea-urchin

One hot day on the beach, when the tide was going out, a big wave swept a helpless sea-urchin off the sea-bed and into a rock pool far up on the beach. When he realized where he was, he stretched his shiny brown spines in the warm, shallow water, and decided to enjoy his adventure.

But as the sun climbed high in the sky, he realised to his horror that his small pool was getting smaller as it gradually dried out. Already his spines were half out of the water, shrivelling in the burning sunshine. Poor little sea-urchin! He knew he couldn't last until the tide returned to cover him again.

Just then a boy passed by and noticed the little urchin in the sand. Using a spade, the boy lifted the sea-urchin and threw him far out into the deep, cooling sea. Now he was safe!

129

14 July
The happy gnomes

There was tremendous excitement and activity in gnomeland! Their prince was marrying a wood sprite princess, and all the gnomes were coming to the wedding.

The garden gnomes came, wearing their brilliantly striped costumes of flower colours; and the woodland gnomes were there, in their tall, leafy hats, with the golden-clothed gnomes of the heathland.

The water gnomes were feeling the heat, so they stayed in the lake just wearing their hats, for as long as possible.

The mountain gnomes, wearing their best red suits, had run all the way down the side of the mountain, and their feet were terribly hot and dusty; so the water gnomes invited them to sit on their water-lily leaf, and cool their feet in the lake.

And what gifts they brought, to the wedding! Delicious fresh fish, iced drinks from the mountains, fruit and nuts from the gardens and woodlands; and purple heather from the heathland, to bring the couple luck and happiness!

15 July
The lost appetite

'It's time for lunch, Patrick!' called his mother. 'It's your favourite, fried chicken and chips!'

Patrick had been ill with measles, and his appetite had not yet returned. Now, he could only eat half his meal, because he just wasn't hungry.

That night his parents decided that a week in the country, on a farm, with his uncle and aunt and cousins, might be good for him; so he went there next day.

At first he felt rather shy and strange. But his cousins took him round the farm, collecting the hens' eggs from the laying boxes, visiting the calves in the field, and watching the cows being milked. He was soon very happy, and eating as much as his cousins ate!

When Patrick's parents came to fetch him, he was strong and pink cheeked – what a difference from the week before!

16 July
She loves me, she loves me not!

Brian was standing under a cherry tree in his garden, picking the petals off a tall daisy, one by one, and murmuring quietly: 'She loves me, she loves me not, she loves me, she loves me not . . .' until the last petal came off with 'she loves me!' Then he did the same thing again.

Suddenly, a bunch of cherries hit him on the head. 'Ow! That hurt!' said Brian.

He looked up, and saw a cross-looking fairy standing on a branch, glaring down at him. 'And don't you think it hurts to have your petals pulled off?' she snapped. 'Why are you doing that?'

'Oh, I'm sorry! I didn't mean to hurt the daisies,' said Brian, astonished. 'I'm trying to decide which of two pretty girls to take to the fancy-dress party.'

'Well, take them both then, silly!' said the fairy – and vanished.

Brian *did* invite them both – and they all ate cherries, and had a good time!

131

17 July
The brave crab

One afternoon a little crab was playing on the beach with his friends, without a care in the world. Then, on the top of the cliff above the beach, he caught sight of a group of children, holding buckets and spades, setting off down the path which led to the beach.

'Oh dear!' the little crab thought to himself anxiously, 'I must try to warn all my friends of the danger we're in!'

He scuttled as fast as he could along the beach – sideways, of course, as all crabs move – calling out in a tiny voice, 'Get back into the sea! There are children coming!' But many didn't hear.

A turtle swimming close to the shore saw him. 'Quick! Climb on my back,' he said.

The turtle swam, the crab clicked his claws, and they all escaped in time!

18 July
My boat and I

One day I'll have a sailing boat!
  We'll rush through the waves, or gently
  float,
My boat and I . . .
  I'll hoist her sails and watch them fill,
Then let the wind blow us where it will,
  My boat and I . . .
Where have you been? they'll ask; I'll say,
  Over the sea and far away,
My boat and I . . .

19 July
The nightingale

Once upon a time a little boy had a bad dream when he went to sleep at night. He dreamed that a fierce two-headed monster was chasing him, and he woke up feeling very frightened.

But when he heard the sweet song of a nightingale outside his window, he forgot his fears and fell peacefully asleep.

20 July
A holiday week

On Monday I went off to play
  With Jane, who lives a mile away.
On Tuesday when the wind was strong,
  I flew my kite the whole day long.
On Wednesday it rained and poured;
  I read my book, and felt quite bored.
On Thursday it was fine again,
  So I went bicycling with Jane.
On Friday I had work to do,
  Helping Mother, and shopping too.
Then Saturday, when Father's free
  To stay at home, and chat with me.
Now Sunday's here! It's my last day
  Of one short week of holiday!

21 July
Off to town!

'What are you grumbling about, Patch?' said Shep, the old sheep dog, to the younger farm dog. Their kennels were close together in the farmyard. 'Don't tell me you're planning to go off and leave us again?' Patch had set off on two previous occasions, but had returned both times the next morning.

'Yes! I'm off, and this time it's for good!' barked Patch. 'I'm tired of living here on the farm in a rough kennel, being woken early every morning, seven days a week, by that noisy cockerel, to go and help bring the cows in for milking.

'And in the day I don't get much rest; if the hens stray, I have to fetch them; if the farmer has work to do, I have to go with him; in the evening, I have to help with the cows again; and all night I'm supposed to be on guard duty, ready to bark if any stranger comes. What a life eh? I don't know how you put up with it, year after year.'

'I'm happy here,' barked Shep. 'The farmer is kind, and I like herding sheep.'

'Well, I've had enough,' yapped Patch. 'What's more, my friend Lulu, who sometimes visits us here, says I can go and live with them in town. She sleeps on a cushion in a basket, in a warm room, and only goes for walks when it's fine. Her job is to fetch her master's slippers! Goodbye, Shep!' He ran off quietly.

Do you think he returned next day?

23 July
The silly hen

There was once a hen who laid her egg every day in the laying box. But one day a little idea came into her head.

'If I could make my own nest outside the hen-run, in a secret place, the farmer's wife wouldn't be able to take my egg every day. Then they might hatch out into chickens!' she thought.

She found a gap in the netting, and soon made a rough nest in some dead grass under the hedge, where she laid her eggs.

But after three days she found a weasel eating her eggs, and ran home as fast as she could. 'I prefer the farmer's wife,' she thought. 'At least, she gives me food!'

22 July
Lost and found

The woodland creatures were all terribly worried. 'Oh dear! He's lost! Where *can* he be?' they chirped, squeaked and grunted in their different voices. 'We can't possibly play hide-and-seek until he's found; perhaps a thief has stolen him!'

They were talking about the cuckoo, who had become rather bold lately, sometimes flying across the fields to the farm.

So the woodpecker, the blackbirds and the finches flew over the fields to the farm, while the fieldmice and moles searched in the wood for their friend.

One of the fieldmice ran across a bare foot! It belonged to Tom, the farm boy, who had fallen asleep under an oak tree. The cuckoo was perching above.

'Ssh! Don't wake him,' said the cuckoo. 'He's my friend too!'

24 July
Flip takes a trip

Ian was getting very excited. His father was a scientist who had spent the last two months living and working in the Arctic Circle, where there is always snow and ice. Now, he had written to say he was coming home on holiday, and would bring Ian a present.

'I wonder what he'll bring!' thought Ian. 'Maybe a sledge; or a snowman.'

His father had been living in a camp, where there were no shops, so he had planned to take a trip to town on his last day and buy something special for Ian. But bad weather was on its way, and the plane came a day early.

As he went to catch the plane, a little waddling figure joined him; it was Flip, the penguin who had become his pet!

'You'd better come too!' said Ian's father. 'Ian will like you very much!'

25 July
Under the water

Miranda had been lying on her tummy by the lakeside for some time. She knew how to swim, but she could not swim *under* the water to the bottom of the lake, and she badly wanted to know what lay there.

'At the bottom of the sea, mermaids live in glistening rocky palaces, decorated with coral and beautiful seashells, with seaweed curtains,' Miranda said to herself. 'They go for drives in their sea-anemone carriages, pulled by prancing sea-horses . . .' PLOP! She was interrupted by a big fish, who suddenly appeared in front of her, and blew a large bubble.

'Step inside, and I'll show you what lies at the bottom of our lake,' he said.

She curled up inside the bubble, and sank down, down, down, until she rested beside . . . Farmer Jones's rusty old car!

The bubble floated upwards again and popped on the surface. Miranda swam ashore and vowed not to be so curious again!

26 July
Off into space!

Roger had been watching a film about some people flying in a space ship. Now it was bedtime, but he didn't feel at all sleepy.

'Try counting sheep,' suggested his mother, as she went to settle him down for the third time.

'Sheep are boring; they never do anything exciting, like going to the moon in a rocket,' grumbled Roger.

'Well, why don't you pretend you're in a rocket, travelling through space, and see how many stars you pass,' said his mother, trying to be helpful. Roger said nothing, so she kissed him and went out.

Roger was wondering whether in fact a rocket would go fast enough for him to pass any stars at all – probably not, he guessed; so that idea wouldn't work.

Then he had a great idea: supposing he could go in a space ship, and then somehow catch hold of a shooting star, find out what happens to them, and write a book about it! Then he'd be famous . . .

When Roger's mother looked in, he was fast asleep.

27 July
Pedro trots home

Pedro, the donkey, had plodded all the way to market early that morning, with the baskets on his back full of fruit. His master had succeeded in selling all the fruit for a good price by midday. Now he could afford a glass of wine with his friends, before returning home.

But while he did this, Pedro managed to slip his bridle off, and trot home! How he laughed with his friend Peppi, the dog, to think he was home before his master!

28 July
Peter's night out

One fine, clear night Peter was returning home after dark with his mother, after visiting friends. He had never seen the stars looking so bright.

'Look! There goes a shooting star,' he said. 'I wish I could catch one, and see what it looks like; I'd give it to you as a present!'

'Oh, what a lovely idea!' said his mother, smiling. 'I never heard of anyone catching a star, but I would like one.'

They walked past the lake. Peter could hardly believe his eyes; there, in the water, he could see lots of stars! He wondered if they were shooting stars that had fallen in, and quickly made a plan.

Later that night, he crept out in the bright moonlight with his little fishing rod, to catch a star for his mother. She found him there asleep, next morning, with Bimbo, the dog, keeping him warm!

29 July
The sparrows

Once upon a time there were two pretty little sparrows, with brown bodies and grey wings, who decided to build a nest together and raise a family. But what they could not decide on, was where they should build their nest.

So they flew all over the countryside, trying to find a suitable place that they could both agree on, and chirping loudly to each other.

'Here's a good place,' said Mr Sparrow, 'under this bridge, over the river; it would be sheltered from the rain.'

'What? And risk our babies falling into the water, and drowning?' said Mrs Sparrow. So they flew on.

'What about this thick beech hedge, dividing two gardens?' suggested Mrs Sparrow. 'We could get plenty of scraps from both families if we built our nest here.' But they saw a big grey cat, prowling on a lawn, and quickly flew away.

At last they agreed on a fine tree by the edge of a wood, close to a waterfall.

They quickly built the nest out of twigs, dried grass and moss, and lined it with feathers. Six eggs were laid, the babies were hatched, grew up, and flew away.

Next year, it was their turn to find good, safe places to build nests!

30 July
The dragonfly

Many children believe in fairies. But Robin not only believed in them, he was always trying to find them! He did not expect to find any in the town where he lived, but if he went with his family to the country, he spent a lot of time searching – for fairies!

One Saturday, after they had picnicked by the side of a lake, Robin's father was woken from his afternoon siesta by having a jam jar thrust under his nose.

'Look! A fairy! I've caught one at last!' A brilliant blue, shimmering, fluttering creature was indeed a prisoner in the jar.

'It's a dragonfly! It won't live if you keep it,' said Robin's father. What a disappointment for poor Robin!

31 July
Two's company . . .

Tallula, the tortoise, was great friends with Kim, the old English sheep-dog. This was perhaps strange, when you consider how different they were!

Tallula was about the size of your hand, spread wide, with a hard shell, and small leathery feet and head which she hid under her shell if she felt that any danger threatened her.

Kim, on the other hand, was a huge, bouncy, friendly, shaggy dog.

For some reason, Tallula did not trust Tompkin, the cat, and always hid her head inside her shell when she saw Tompkin coming. The cat would touch the tortoise's shell gently with her paw, as though she wasn't sure if anyone was hiding underneath. But Tallula always waited until Tompkin was some distance away before she continued her stroll.

'Mmm! I'll eat that,' Tallula would think, as she spotted a juicy slug. Kim would bound up in his friendly way, jump over Tallula and sniff the slug. Tallula never minded. She sometimes had a sleep with her giant friend, between his paws!

'Here's your dinner, Kim! And milk, Tallula!' The two friends ate and drank happily, side by side, on the lawn.

1 August
The wounded lamb

It was Jimmy's turn to run and find a hiding place, while his sisters, Caroline and Linda, counted to twenty, with their eyes closed. Linda was younger, so she counted to ten, and Caroline continued.

'COMING!' they both called, and started searching behind the bushes and trees. After a few minutes, they heard a faint 'Coo-ee!' and followed the sound to an old shed, where they found Jimmy and . . . a wounded lamb! It had a bad scratch on its leg, and was too weak to stand.

Caroline and Linda ran home and fetched a bottle of water with disinfectant in it, cotton wool, a bandage and safety pins, and warmed milk and water for the lamb to drink. Soon, it was strong enough to walk.

The farmer was so grateful, he let them have its fleece, when it was shearing time!

2 August
Rufus's hedgehog

Rufus was a little boy with red hair. He lived on the edge of a forest which was full of animals and birds. Rufus spent a lot of his time in the forest, learning about the animals, and playing with them.

He used to put fresh lettuce leaves down, and crumbs, and a saucer of milk, and then sit and wait for the rabbits, birds, and hedgehog family to come and find the food.

One day mother and father hedgehog didn't turn up – only the baby, who seemed very hungry and sad. The same thing happened next day.

'Perhaps they were run over on the road beside the forest,' thought Rufus. 'I'll look after him until he's old enough to fend for himself.' So he carried the little hedgehog on his back in a rucksack, while he found the right food for him; then he took him home.

After two weeks, Rufus let the hedgehog go; but he still came back for rides!

3 August
The timid fawn

It was a beautiful day. The mother deer tenderly licked Mandy, her baby, who was snuggled up close beside her.

'It's time you went for a little walk on your own,' whispered the doe.

'Tweet! Tweet! Come with me, and I'll look after you,' twittered the blue tit. So off they went together, Mandy stepping lightly on her thin, delicate legs, while the little bird flew ahead.

'Oh,' breathed the rabbits, 'what a beautiful fawn! Will you play with us?'

'Look out!' grunted the badger, and the animals all rushed to safety. Mandy took eight bounds to reach her mother's side.

'It's the wild cat,' explained the badger. 'It wants to catch the blue tit.'

Mandy's father, the stag, chased it away with his antlers. They were safe again.

4 August
The lake fairy

One fine, summer's night, the fairy of the lake went to visit her friend, the fairy of the forest. Coming back through the forest she lost the way. It was getting late – only half an hour from sunrise – and the fairy of the lake knew that unless she reached her home before the first rays of the sun touched the peak of the distant mountain, she would be turned into a waterfall.

A tortoise offered to show her the way home, but he couldn't get her there quickly enough. What should she do?

She looked up at the sky. Already it was getting light, but one star remained, faintly shining.

'I *wish* I could get home in time,' she murmured. All at once a shooting star sped across the sky and hovered, low. The fairy followed, and was soon safe in the cool depths of her watery home.

5 August
The windmill

The windmill on top of the hill was bored. There had been no wind for three days, and he had nothing to do except stand with his four sails outstretched, enviously watching the sparrows flying around. They felt sorry for him.

One clever sparrow had an idea. 'If we all perched on the top of one sail, maybe our weight would be enough to get you turning again,' he chirped.

So he flew all round the countryside collecting as many sparrows as he could find. When they all perched on one of the windmill's sails, he started to turn!

'How kind of you to take all this trouble!' said the windmill, happily.

'It's fun!' said the sparrows. 'May we come again tomorrow?'

7 August
Pom's big catch

The river was teaming with salmon, and the lucky bears who lived in the forest near its banks were able to fish them out of the water quite easily with their paws.

But Pom, the bear cub, didn't find it so easy. He either dipped his paw in the water clumsily, so the fish got away, or he overbalanced and fell in, frightening away all the fish and annoying the bears.

One day he was strolling by the river bank when he came across some fishermen. They rushed away in terror, dropping their rods; so Pom picked one up, cast the line and . . . hey presto! He caught a salmon! And then another! When he had six, he took them home, and was voted champion salmon fisher of the forest!

6 August
Where's the wolf?

It was very early in the morning. Barney, the rabbit, was waiting at home for his friend Otto, the otter, who was supposed to be coming with him on a fishing trip.

'He's late,' grumbled Barney. 'What can have kept him?'

Just then, he caught sight of his old enemy, the fox, slinking past the window, trying not to be seen. Then a knock came at the door, and a muffled voice called out, 'Here I am, Barney.'

'That sly rogue overheard our plan; I'll teach him a lesson,' thought Barney.

He draped an old wolf-skin rug right over himself, and opened the door. The fox was terrified and ran away, howling.

A minute later there was another knock at the door, and this time it was Otto.

'You're late,' said Barney. But the poor otter fainted at the sight of a wolf!

8 August
Gino's oasis

'When I grow up, I'm going to be a big, clever genie like Daddy,' said Gino, the little genie of the desert. 'He can make a lot of magic things happen, but I can only do a few tricks.'

'We'll give you a test, to see if you can use your head as well as your magic powers,' smiled his magic teacher. 'Take this handful of dates and this flask of water, and see how long you can manage to stay out in the burning desert.'

Off went Gino the same evening, into the hot desert. He knew he couldn't stay long unless he thought of something. He dug a hole in the sand, put the dates in it, and watered them from his flask. In the cool night, the dates opened and took root; by morning tall date palms had grown up!

Gino dug with his hands to get back some of his water, and a fresh spring bubbled up. Now he could stay there a long time!

In the old days they harvested the corn differently from nowadays.

Quite early in the morning everyone made their way to the cornfield with the old mare pulling the reaper. The children skipped along, pushing each other and laughing, while the women chatted, their rakes in their hands. The men walked more quietly, some smoking pipes, with long coils of twine over their shoulders.

There was the field of ripe corn, stretching away into the distance. The reaper started its work, going up and down, cutting the corn and leaving it in neat piles, row upon row. The children followed, neatly laying the twine – now cut into lengths tied round their waists – by each pile.

Then the women placed the corn on the twine with their rakes, for the men to tie into sheaves.

How peaceful and friendly those harvests seem, compared with noisy, modern machines!

9 August
Lady scarecrow!

'Those crows are eating up all my corn!' shouted the farmer angrily. 'I'll soon put a stop to that!' He stumped off to the barn and fetched an old scarecrow. The rats had taken most of its old clothes for making their nests, so he took an old coat and hat of his wife's, dressed the scarecrow and put him in the field.

'That'll scare them,' said the farmer, grinning. 'They'll think it's my wife!'

At first the crows weren't sure who this new creature was; but one bold bird swooped down close and glanced under the brim.

'Come back, everyone,' he cawed. 'It's only the old straw scarecrow, wearing a lady's hat. What a silly sight!'

'If you're going to make rude remarks, I shall go back to the barn,' said the scarecrow, feeling quite upset.

'No, please stay; you are our friend!' cawed the crow, and perched on his arm.

147

11 August
Peter's fish

In Peter's garden there was a pond, fed by a little stream, and surrounded by flowers. It was Peter's favourite place to play.

One day he made himself a little rod and line with a stick and some string, fixed some left-over food on a bent pin for bait, and went to try his luck fishing in the pond. He lay down and fell asleep.

When he woke, he found a beautiful fish caught on the line. 'Hooray!' he thought. 'I can give it to Mummy as a present!' But when he picked up the fish, it looked at him so miserably that he felt sorry for it, unhooked the pin from its mouth and threw it back into the water. He picked a bunch of flowers, hoping his mother would prefer flowers to fish!

12 August
The sand castle

The tide was out when Alison and Roger arrived on the beach in the morning.

'Let's build the best sand castle in the world!' shouted Roger.

They collected beautiful shells of different shapes and sizes, and then spent a long time making a splendid sand castle.

'Well done, you two!' called their mother. 'You deserve ice-creams now!'

The children met some friends at the ice-cream van, and stayed to play. When they returned the tide had crept up and washed away their lovely castle!

'We'll make another tomorrow,' said Roger.

13 August
The apricots

Mrs Dingle was old and lived alone. Her young neighbour Katy often went shopping for her, and Mrs Dingle was very grateful.

One day Katy knocked on her door and offered her a big basket of delicious apricots from their garden.

'Oh, thank you dear,' she said. 'I'd like to *borrow* them until tomorrow, if I may!'

Next day, she gave Katy four pots of apricot jam, as thanks for her kindness!

14 August
The bumble bee

Carolyn was playing in the garden near her mother, in the afternoon sunshine.

'I'm hot,' she said, with a sigh.

'Go and help yourself to a peach from the kitchen', said her mother.

When Carolyn reached out to take one, a big bumble bee flew out of the basket, and gave her an awful fright.

'Bumble bees don't sting,' said Mummy. 'Perhaps he was feeling hot too!'

15 August
Toby's concert

Poor Melanie! Although it was the middle of summer, she had somehow managed to catch a bad cold, and was not allowed to play in the garden with her brother Toby. She had to stay in her room and rest for the afternoon, alone – except for her dolls and her teddy bear.

'It's not fair!' she grumbled. 'I'm better today than I was yesterday.'

Then she heard Toby's voice, coming through her window. He was singing all the funny songs he could think of and strumming his guitar. Soon she was laughing happily; and she made her dolls dance to the music!

16 August
Planting roses

One day young Reggie Rabbit decided it was time he had some roses growing in his garden. His neighbour had given him a big bunch of pink roses that morning, so he took some outside, dug little holes for them with a trowel, and planted them.

'Look!' he said proudly to some birds who flew over to see what he was doing. 'This rain will help them to grow.'

'But look at the rainbow, Reggie!' the birds chirped. 'The hot sun will soon make your roses shrivel up and die!'

Reggie put the roses in a vase indoors, and went round to ask his neighbour how he grew such beautiful rose bushes!

17 August
The lonely spring

At the foot of a beautiful pink flowering bush a spring bubbled up from the ground and ran away as a clear, sparkling stream. The bush grew big quickly, because even in hot dry weather its roots could always find moisture from the spring.

But the spring was lonely. 'Although I keep murmuring and gurgling all day and all night long, nobody ever talks to me,' it complained. 'The bulrushes just sway gently on their stiff stems; and *you* can't talk to me, can you?' it asked the pretty flowering bush. A flurry of pink petals fell into the clear water, as the bush sadly shook its head.

Just then, a stork flew overhead, with a frog caught by one leg in its beak. The frog wriggled free and *plop!* fell into the spring below. He swam to the bank and sat there, croaking happily. At last, the spring had someone who would talk to it!

18 August
A sunshine song

Sally loved singing. She was good at it too, and sang in tune. She learned all the nursery rhymes that were set to music, like Sing a Song of Sixpence, Jack and Jill, Hickory Dickory Dock and lots of others, and could sing them all the way through without any difficulty.

'Why don't you make up new words to an old tune?' suggested her mother. Next day, Sally sang this song:

Sing a song of sunshine,
    Summer's here at last!
Flowers in the garden
    Tell us spring is past.
Picnics in the country,
    Swimming in the sea,
Holidays are happy days,
    So sing this song with me!

19 August
Billy's picture

Billy came back from school with something important to tell his mother.

'My teacher says we're going to have a competition,' he said. 'I have to paint a picture, and take it to school. What's a competition?'

'It's when each person tries to do something better than the others,' smiled his mother. 'Sometimes there's a prize.'

'I want to paint my picture now,' said Billy. He got out his pencil, paints and paint brush, and settled down at the table in front of a big white sheet of paper, thinking of what he would do.

First he drew a shepherd with some sheep and a sheep dog. Then he drew the shepherd's house, with smoke coming out of the chimney, and a tree with a bird singing in the garden. A butterfly, some flowers – and it was ready for colouring.

Next week, Billy came home from school with some paints; he had won first prize!

20 August
The shelter

Jennie and her brother Ben set off one summer morning for the woods. They took with them a bag of crumbs and left-over scraps, a picnic for themselves, and another bag containing nails and a hammer.

They found a pleasant grassy clearing, and put their bags down. 'Now, to work!' said Ben. They searched around for small broken-off branches, and twigs, and put them in neat piles of the same sizes.

For the next half hour there was much tapping and banging, fetching and carrying, fitting and fixing, until the children had finished their work. There in front of them stood a fine, sturdy little shelter, just big enough for their small woodland friends – the birds, fieldmice and perhaps rabbits – to come under.

Jennie and Ben ate their picnic, watching their friends eat in the shelter!

21 August
Cakes of soap!

Rosie was so pleased! It was market day in the town near where they lived, and her grandmother had invited her to go with her.

'Bring your friend Kay, if you like,' said Granny, 'then you can look round the market together while I shop.'

What fun to trot through the lanes in a little trap drawn by a donkey! The girls loved the journey, and thoroughly enjoyed wandering round the market, buying a few things with pocket-money.

They returned to the trap, and found a basket tucked under the seat. 'Let's look inside!' said Rosie; they each took out what looked like a cake, and bit into it.

'Ugh! It's soap!' gasped Rosie.

Her grandmother returned, and laughed. 'Here's some *real* cake for you!' she said.

22 August
A trip to to the sea

One beautiful sunny day, Nicola decided to take her pet rabbit Tim down to the beach. He had never been to the sea.

She put a toy sunhat on his head, with holes cut for his ears, and put him in her bicycle basket. Then off they went.

'Oh, Tim, you don't know what a treat is in store for you!' she said to the rabbit, who didn't know what was happening.

When they got to the beach, Nicola undressed very quickly and carried Tim to the sea. She put him in the shallow water, but a wave went up his nose and he sneezed loudly, wriggled free, and ran into the sand dunes! When Nicola had had a swim, she went to look for him.

She soon found Tim, happily digging tunnels in the soft sand! 'It's the sand you like – not the sea!' laughed Nicola.

23 August
The space fairy

Some people say there is a space fairy, who lives way up high in the sky. He stretches a silver moonbeam between two stars, and does clever tricks and dances on it, like a tight-rope walker at the circus. As he leaps and twirls, out of his magic umbrella falls the golden light of summer, on to our Earth below.

He keeps watch over the baby space fairy, asleep in her crescent moon cradle, while the stars and planets twinkle and turn like mobiles in a child's bedroom.

Towards the end of summer he leaves his moonbeam tight-rope, jumps on to the back of a shooting star, and searches for autumn colours to bring back in his magic umbrella and scatter over the world.

156

24 August
Kind Ophelia

Ophelia was a pretty girl, with long golden coloured hair which was thick and wavy, rather like a mermaid's hair.

In the summer she spent hours on the seashore every day alone, collecting empty shells to make into necklaces and bracelets, paddling in the shallow water, and walking along the beach and over the rocks.

The other children sometimes caught tiny crabs, starfish and live shellfish and kept them in their buckets. If Ophelia found any, she threw them as far as she could, back into the sea, where they belonged. This made the children cross.

One day, so the story goes, Ophelia found a baby dolphin stranded on the beach at high tide. She managed to get it back into the sea, saving its life. The fairy of the sea was so grateful, she came and touched Ophelia with her magic wand, turning her for an hour into a mermaid, to swim, and ride happily on the back of her new dolphin friend.

25 August
Pumpkin soup

A round, ripe pumpkin had been loaded into the farmer's cart. As the horse pulled the cart up the stony track, the pumpkin jiggled and joggled about, getting closer and closer to the back.

'If I wriggle a bit more, I can escape, and roll back to my nice comfortable bed,' thought the pumpkin.

A final heave got him off the back of the cart, rolling down the track which passed his old vegetable patch.

'Oh dear! I can't stop,' gasped the pumpkin, beginning to feel dizzy as he rolled faster and faster down the slope.

SPLASH! He rolled into a large puddle, giving a gosling a dreadful fright, and surprising the donkey drinking there.

'Hee-haw!' You should be made into soup!' brayed the donkey; and that is just what the farmer's wife did!

27 August
Rudy is lost

Rudy was a very young kangaroo, who lived in his mother's pouch. One day, he managed to slip out without his mother noticing, and in a few bounds he was free – for the very first time!

'Where are you going?' asked the koala bear, up in a tree. 'Does your mother know you're here alone?'

'Oh yes; I often go for walks on my own,' Rudy lied, and bounded away.

'Look out!' screeched a parrot. 'There's a sand storm blowing up.' Soon Rudy couldn't see anything. He was lost!

Then he felt himself being picked up and put to bed. His mother had found him!

26 August
The hunting trip

A little Indian boy got up one morning, and said, 'Mother, today I am taking my canoe up the river on a hunting expedition. I shall bring food back for our supper tonight. Don't worry about me – I shall not be alone.'

His mother knew he was a sensible boy, so she gave him food for the day and let him go. 'Come back before sunset,' she said.

The little Indian boy pushed off in his canoe and paddled hard upstream, against the current. He wasn't alone for long! An otter soon swam up, and gave him a fish as a present! He steered the canoe towards the bank, and went to visit some beavers who were building a dam. They gave him wild berries which they had collected, and in return, he helped them with their work.

As he was leaving for home, a friendly raccoon brought him a gift of eggs.

'You are an excellent hunter!' said his mother when he gave her everything.

The little Indian boy smiled!

28 August
Dimple's boast

Dimple was a fine, strong young donkey. But unfortunately, he was always boasting about how big and strong he was.

'I'm as strong as an . . . an . . . elephant!' he said one day, not sure what that was.

But his wise old uncle Isaac knew, and he quickly said, 'Elephants can carry people on their heads! Let's see if you can even manage a basket!' He picked up a big basket of fruit in his mouth, and put it on Dimple's head. Soon his head drooped under the weight, and the fruit rolled all over the ground. Poor Dimple was smacked, and he never boasted again!

29 August
Poor Mrs Mouse

Poor Mrs Mouse was in quite a state! Like the old woman who lived in a shoe, she had so many children she didn't know what to do. And not only that, all her baby mice had stayed playing out in the sun too long, and they all had headaches and had to stay in bed with the curtains drawn.

'Oh dear, what shall I do?' she sobbed. 'There is no food in the house, and I can't leave them alone to go shopping when they're not well, and crying for me.'

A little bird heard her, and he flew off and told some of her friends.

In a very short time there was a soft whirring of wings, a gentle buzzing sound, and a little knock at Mrs Mouse's front door. There stood Mrs Bee with a honeycomb, Mrs Butterfly with some butter, and Miss Dragonfly with bread and cakes. Mrs Mouse didn't know how to thank them!

30 August
Magic butterfly

Sylvia had been watching a butterfly in the garden. It flew towards her, and then flew away and settled on a flower. Back to her it fluttered, then away to another flower.

'Why does it do that?' wondered Sylvia. She stood up, walked over to where it was, and scooped it into her cupped hands. It opened its wings flat, then closed them again – like a wink!

Suddenly, Sylvia felt herself shrinking until she was the same size as the butterfly. She jumped on its back, and away they flew to a magic land where everything had changed size! She danced a polka with a bear cub, in and out of the flowers.

The trees had shrunk, and a giant snail waved its great horns at her . . . then Sylvia woke in the garden! The butterfly had gone.

31 August
Percy in America

Here is a story which tells how penguins were all white once upon a time, and then changed their colouring.

Percy, the young penguin, rubbed his little flippers together to warm up after a swim in the icy water. He couldn't see any of his friends, so he decided to creep up behind a sea-lion who was watching a hole in the ice for fish, and throw a snow ball at him. But the sea-lion heard him and swept Percy into the sea with a flick of his strong tail.

Percy landed on the back of a dolphin. He hung on, and was carried all the way to the warm waters off the coast of Florida. There the sun was so strong that everyone's skin was suntanned and dark. Percy's back turned black – though his tummy remained as white as the snow he had left behind him.

And that is how penguins look today!

1 September
The garden fairy and the mist fairy

Amalinda was a garden fairy, pink from head to toe. She lived in a sunny garden, full of roses and other pretty flowers.

One morning, as she gazed into her crystal ball – which was a dew-drop – she saw something which she could hardly believe; she saw a village, shrouded in mist, where the sun couldn't shine and the flowers were imprisoned in their buds because there was no warmth to make them bloom! Amalinda immediately sent her bird messenger to find out what was wrong. He was soon back again with the answer.

'The birds there say that the fairy of the autumn mists was woken early from her summer sleep by a cold wind in the mountains. Now she wanders round the village, spreading clouds of mist, and giving everyone the shivers!'

'Something must be done,' said Amalinda. 'I know summer's nearly over, but autumn is not yet here.' Waving her magic wand, she called a warm breeze, and said, 'Go to the misty village, and gently blow, the mist fairy back to the mountains! And kind sun, shine warmly on the flower buds!'

Next day, she heard that the village was sunny again, and the flowers were out!

2 September
Summer lament

Summer's nearly over,
  Long hot days are past.
Evenings now feel chilly,
  Light is falling fast.

Harvests should be gathered,
  Grain is stored away.
Field are full of stubble,
  Ricks are high with hay.

Swallows have departed,
Following the sun;
They can't stay through winter,
  Snow and ice they shun!

Summer's nearly ended,
  How long till the next?
Nine long months to wait now –
  No use feeling vexed!

3 September
Blackberry jam

Old Mr Hedgehog could feel it in his bones. 'It's autumn; that's what it is,' he said to himself, leaning out of the window of his house, sniffing the early morning air. 'I'm late making blackberry jam this year, and I must tidy up my house and leave it clean before I go to sleep for the winter. *And* there's wood to collect for the fire, in case the evenings start to get cold. I must get to work!'

While he was out gathering blackberries, some young rabbits who had seen him in the summer, slowly going about his own business, hopped over to speak to him.

'You're in a hurry Mr Hedgehog; anything wrong?' said one.

'You rabbits don't have to stock up your houses for the winter as I do,' he explained. 'I'm late making jam, and I haven't any sugar.' The rabbits ran off.

When he got home, he found a wild honeycomb on his table. 'That's better than sugar for making jam,' he said happily.

4 September
Nico the lion cub

Nico the baby lion cub was very curious. And as well as wanting to know about everything, he was also disobedient.

'What's over there, beyond that tall grass at the edge of the jungle?' he asked.

'There's a village with huts, where men live,' answered the lioness.

'I'd like to see that,' said Nico.

'No, don't go near it! Men can be very dangerous,' warned his mother.

But, being inquisitive, of course Nico had to go and have a look.

He crept as quietly as he could through the long grass, but suddenly . . . *crackle, crackle, THUD!* He had fallen through a light covering of branches and leaves into a hole. It was a trap, made by men.

'Mummy! Here's a lion cub! I want to play with him,' shouted a little boy.

After that Nico played with the boy every day, in the village. They were not afraid of each other. They were friends.

5 September
Signs of autumn

Sarah and Jim were back at school again after a lovely holiday by the sea with their parents. They lived in a big city, and now they had to get used to wearing ordinary clothes again, after swimsuits!

They were very pleased when their aunt and uncle invited them down to the country their first weekend back in town.

First they showed off their suntans.

'I've learnt to do doggy-paddle *and* breast-stroke,' said Sarah proudly, 'and just look at my collection of shells!'

Jim wanted to go for a walk. 'See how many signs of autumn you can both bring back,' suggested his uncle.

They found leaves turning to gold, beech nuts, acorns – and some spotted toadstools.

'Those are poisonous,' said their uncle. 'You should throw them away and wash your hands!' They had learnt something new.

6 September
The tea-party

Annette decided it was time she had a dolls' tea-party. So she invited three of her friends to come and help.

First they fetched the toy chairs and table which Daddy had made for Annette's last birthday, and put them in the garden. Then they carefully laid the table with the dolls' tea-set – four cups, saucers and plates, a tea-pot, milk jug and sugar bowl. They put paint in water to make tea, flour in water for milk, and flour for sugar. They made jam sandwiches with leaves and flower petals, and pebbles made good biscuits and cakes.

Big Bear, Golly, Jemima Rag-Doll and Baby Doll were all dressed in their best, and sat round the table. What a feast!

When the party was over, Mummy called them. They ran inside, and found the table stacked with their favourite food – and this time, it was real!

7 September
The stork's nest

Hans lived in a place called Alsace, on the east side of France. Visitors to his village often stopped to admire his house, with its window-boxes full of scarlet geraniums, and the beautiful dark beams making a criss-cross pattern against the white walls. This made Hans feel very proud.

But the thing that made him proudest of all was the storks' nest, perched high up on top of the chimney. This year, two baby storks had been born there, right on top of the house!

One morning Hans noticed that the nest was empty. He waited and watched all day, but the storks didn't return. 'Why have they gone?' he asked his mother sadly.

'They don't like our cold winters,' she told him, 'so they fly to a warmer country, and return in spring.' Hans was pleased.

165

9 September
Lullaby

Hush-a-bye, baby,
    Mother is here;
Stars in the sky say
    Dreaming time's near!

Columbine's sleeping,
    So is Pierrot,
Snuggled up warmly,
    Close to the doe.

8 September
Greg's horse

'Oo, look Mummy! There's a funfair!'

Greg was out shopping with his mother. They had just got off the bus, when Greg noticed roundabouts, flashing lights and loud, twangy music.

'There's my friend Pete! Please, let me go and have some rides!'

His mother agreed to let him go for half an hour while she shopped, and gave him five coins. 'Stay with Pete,' she said.

When she came back, he was riding a fine dapple grey horse on the roundabout.

'What did you like best?' asked Mummy.

'I bought a stick of barley-sugar, and rode my horse all the time,' smiled Greg.

10 September
Bright-Eyes

Little Bright-Eyes was Mother Rabbit's youngest child. As well as being the smallest, he was also the liveliest, and was never afraid. He liked to leave the edge of the forest, where their burrow was, and pay visits to the cows in the next door field, showing them how high he could jump and how fast he could run.

Poor Mother Rabbit tried to make her son take greater care. 'If you run about in the open so much, the fox will catch you – or men with guns will come and shoot you.' But he took no notice.

She went to ask advice from the fairy of the forest.

'As it is springtime,' said the fairy, 'I will mix a magic green paint, made with ferns, mosses and leaves, which will turn his coat green and give him a camouflage.'

Mother Rabbit was very grateful, and painted the mixture on Bright-Eyes, who became almost invisible in the fields.

When summer came, and he played in the cornfields, she went again to the fairy of the forest who mixed a magic yellow paint from golden gorse flowers. This gave him a new camouflage.

In autumn, he wore paint made from horse chestnuts and bracken; and in winter, when it snowed, he wore paint mixed from puff-balls and mistletoe berries.

Lucky Bright-Eyes was safe all year!

11 September
The concert

All the insects who were musical had been invited to come and rehearse before giving a concert.

A large black beetle was in charge. He decided who could take part in the concert, and he was also the conductor.

First the crickets bustled in, sat down and chirrupped loudly.

'Yes, yes! Very good! That's enough, thank you,' said the beetle. 'Next please.'

Next came the grasshoppers who made a buzzing sort of music. 'Quite nice,' said the beetle, 'but tune up first, please!'

A bluebottle droned out his tune, flying round and round. 'Can't you play sitting down?' asked the beetle. The bluebottle shook its head.

Just at that moment in flew several bees and wasps, who all flew round and round the beetle's head, buzzing and droning in loud close harmony.

The beetle tapped his stick for silence.

'Bees, fly round and round; wasps and bluebottle, fly to and fro. That's better.'

The concert was a great success. A dragonfly joined in, whirring its wings, and a ladybird was allowed to do a tap-dance on a leaf. It was a very quiet tap-dance – but she did look so charming!

12 September
The bowl of nuts

Diana was sitting at a table, a pencil in her hand, a few curved lines on a large sheet of drawing paper, and a bowl of nuts on the table in front of her. It was hard getting the curve of the bowl exactly right; she screwed up her eyes and held her pencil out in front of her, as she had seen older people do.

Everything seemed to go blurry, and the largest nut opened silently, allowing a fairy to climb out and fly up above the bowl. She placed a tiny whistle to her lips and blew a shrill blast.

There was a sound rather like popcorn exploding. Before Diana's eyes all the nuts opened and out jumped lots of merry imps, some dressed all in red, others in green. One of the red imps had a blue football which he kicked to another, then it went to another . . . but now the greens had it!

'Come on, greens!' shouted Diana, banging the table with her fists, making the bowl jump. She looked carefully at it, measured it with her pencil, and got on with her drawing. All was quiet again.

13 September
The helper

Mrs Mouse was a busy little person. But she was so kind that she could never resist doing a good turn when she felt one was needed. 'Perhaps I'll be the one who needs help next time,' she would say.

One day she met a frog limping. 'Why aren't you jumping?' she asked him.

'I've strained the springs in my back legs,' he groaned.

Then she met a snail trying to tuck his horns in. 'What's the matter?' she asked.

'This cold wind makes my horns ache,' he grumbled.

Next she passed a lizard peeping out from his hole in a wall. 'Don't you want to stretch your legs?' she asked him.

'My tail has broken off, and I don't like to let people see me until a new one has grown,' whispered the lizard.

Mrs Mouse went home. She knitted a hat for the snail, made a tail-coat for the lizard, and lent her best walking-stick to the frog, until his springs mended.

She just enjoyed helping people!

14 September
Back to school

'I don't want to go back to school,' said Jo sulkily, after the holidays.

'It'll be fun seeing all your friends again, and swapping news,' said Mummy.

'I don't feel like working,' said Jo.

At school that morning the teacher asked all the children in the class to draw, and then paint an autumn leaf. He said Jo's was very good, and pinned it up.

'I like school,' said Jo, back at home.

15 September
The straw basket

A little girl had just been given a new straw basket with a lid. The old basket with no lid, which she always used to take out shopping, was left hanging on a hook for days on end.

'If only someone would use me, I'd be so happy,' thought the basket. The front door was open, and a coat was pulled roughly off the next hook, causing the basket to swing to and fro. A little heave, and . . . *bump*! On to the floor it jumped, and rolled quickly towards the door. The cat kindly patted it through the doorway, and a big dog, who was passing, picked it up in its mouth and ran to the wood, where he left it.

Mrs Squirrel picked it up. 'That's just what I need for collecting nuts!' she said.

The basket was so happy to be used again!

16 September
Old Mr Bear

'I must be getting short-sighted,' grunted old Mr Bear as he leant on his walking-stick and dabbed a cut above his eye with a rather grubby handkerchief. 'I must have walked right into that branch without seeing it.'

Through the trees he could see Mrs Hedgehog's tiny house. He shuffled slowly over, and bent down to knock at her door.

'My word, you are in a bad way!' cried Mrs Hedgehog. Mr Bear managed to squeeze his head and shoulders through the window, and Mrs Hedgehog bathed the cut, and gave him a cup of tea. Then he shuffled home.

'I'll give her some honey,' he decided.

18 September
Mushrooms

'Let's see how many mushrooms you've picked,' said David, Diana's older brother. 'Oh, you have got a lot! But what are those coloured ones? Where did you find them? They're not mushrooms.'

'They were growing near that rotten old tree stump, at the edge of the wood. They are very pretty,' said Diana.

'Throw them away! They're poisonous. Mushrooms grow in fields, with creamy coloured tops and soft pink gills. Come on! I'll race you home.' They ran back to show what they had picked.

17 September
Baby Kiki

It was a very hot day on the wide, sunny plains where Bertha, the mother kangaroo, lived. She was on her way to visit Granny Kangaroo, but at the slow rate she was going she was afraid it would take her all day to get there.

Granny Kangaroo saw her coming in the distance, and went to meet her.

'Why are you taking such slow, short jumps?' she asked. 'Are you ill?'

'No, I'm just worn out,' sighed Bertha. 'It's my youngest who's the cause of my trouble – little Kiki. Although he's getting quite big and heavy, he still thinks of himself as the baby of the family, and insists on staying in my pouch most of the time, especially if we're travelling! Just look at his cheeky little face peeping out now!'

'I get blisters on my feet; and I like it here, anyway,' said Kiki grumpily.

Granny knitted Kiki a pair of striped cotton socks. He was so proud, he was out all day long, showing them to his friends!

20 September
Winter in Africa

'Why are there so many swallows up there on the wires, making such a chattering noise?' asked Oliver.

'They do that each year, before they fly away,' explained his father, coming to look. 'They'll spend the winter in North Africa, where it's much warmer.'

'Let's go to Africa too,' said Oliver.

'I have to work here, and you have school; they'll be back,' said his father.

19 September
Autumn leaves

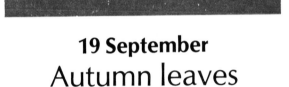

The chestnut leaves were all getting very excited. For days they had been making themselves look beautiful in their dresses of gold, orange and bronze colours, in readiness for the ball. Prince Autumn Wind would be there, to dance with all of them. Of course, each leaf wanted to stay twirling and whirling in the air longer than every other one!

They shivered a little with excitement, as they heard the Prince approaching, saw the branches and twigs bowing before him, and heard the sound of music in the air. Then, *whoosh*! Away they went, twisting and turning in their dance.

Sometimes, children stood under the tree and tried to catch the leaves as they fell, hoping that every leaf caught would bring them a happy month next year!

But most of them would make a golden carpet for the Prince to pass over.

21 September
Bobby's toys

Bobby had been given a beautiful big toy monkey for his second birthday. But that was three whole weeks ago, and he was still sitting on the high shelf in Bobby's bedroom, waiting to be played with.

'Why doesn't that little boy play with me?' he asked the teddy bear plaintively. 'I'm fluffy with bendy arms and legs, and I can hang by my tail and do all sorts of clever tricks. I can't understand why he prefers to play with you, when you've lost half your fur and one eye.'

The teddy bear looked up at the handsome monkey with his one good eye. 'All I can say,' he replied, 'is that if you want to keep your coat clean and glossy, your hands and feet pink, and both your bright round eyes in your head, you'd better not let Bobby play with you! I'm shabby because he always likes playing with me; I go everywhere with him. I don't mind, because I know he loves me best!'

The monkey didn't know whether to stay clean and lonely up on his shelf, or whether to roll over on to the floor for some fun, and risk being spoiled!

22 September
Winter stores

Mrs Hedgehog was worried that they might not have enough food stored away for the winter. 'We haven't any fruit,' she said anxiously. 'It would be lovely to nibble an apple every now and then, if we wake up and feel hungry.'

Little Harry Hedgehog jumped up and down with excitement. 'Mummy, I know where there's a pile of sweet red apples! They belong to an old lady who gives me a saucer of milk when she sees me.'

'Show us the way, son,' grunted Mr Hedgehog. They left the wood, skirted a field, squeezed through a hedge, and there they were, under the apple tree!

'But it's too far to carry the apples!' grumbled Mrs Hedgehog. 'They *do* look good!'

'Watch me!' ordered Mr Hedgehog. He curled up in a ball and rolled on the apples. One stuck to his back, and he trotted off with it. The others copied, and soon they had enough for the winter.

23 September
Blackberry picking

'May we go and pick blackberries?' asked William, looking for a small bowl.

'Oh yes! Please, Mummy,' begged Sandra, 'you know you like making jam!'

'Do I?' smiled their mother. 'I don't think there will be many left, but you can look.' She gave Sandra a bowl.

The children ran and skipped away down the lane, and crossed a field to their favourite place for blackberries.

'Look! There are still plenty,' said William, trying one. 'And they're good!'

When they got back with only a few, the stains round their mouths told their mother the full story. 'It's lucky I've already made plenty of jam!' she said.

24 September
The rhubarb leaves

A fine strong rhubarb plant stood in a vegetable garden. The stalks were a rich shade of red, leading to big, wide green leaves. But the leaves were not happy.

'People come and pull us out of the ground,' they said sadly. 'They cut off our lovely red stalks to make puddings and pies, but they throw us away. We must be easily the finest leaves in the vegetable garden, but no one uses us!'

The sky went dark, clouds gathered and rain began to fall heavily. A bee, loaded with pollen, flew on to a leaf, sheltered by a higher one. A damp butterfly fluttered gratefully under another. And finally, a small marmalade kitten scuttled under the lowest leaf, to keep dry.

The rhubarb plant arched its leaves proudly, happy to be useful at last!

175

25 September
Cheeky Charlie!

One morning cheeky Charlie Shrew stood and watched while a centipede hurried by.

'Excuse me,' he called out, trying not to grin. 'As you have so many feet, do they tread on each other very often?'

'Certainly not! My feet always know exactly where they are,' said the centipede, very offended. 'Tell me, young shrew, as you have such a long tail, do people tread on it very often?' He walked towards Charlie's tail, but Charlie ran off. He never teased the centipede again!

26 September
The wild rabbit

Ben was a wild rabbit. He lived in a sandy burrow amongst heather, silver birch trees and pine trees. He had a happy life with plenty of friends, running free in the woods and moorlands, but he always had to be on the look out for enemies.

If a rabbit sensed danger in the form of a fox, a man, or any big creature, he would drum with his hind legs on the ground, and all the rabbits would dive for cover.

Although he enjoyed eating the grass, wild herbs and plants that grew near his home, he sometimes waited until nightfall and then visited his cousin who lived in a hutch, near a vegetable garden full of delicious carrots and lettuces.

'I have a safe, easy life,' said Ben's fat cousin, looking out through the wire.

Ben twitched his ears, listening for the dog's bark. He was glad he was free.

27 September
The two friends

Josephine the tortoise led a quiet life in a walled garden. One day a boy left the gate open by mistake. Josephine saw her chance to see what the world was like outside. Although home-loving by nature, she decided to go for a walk, and slowly walked out of the garden unnoticed – or so she thought.

Into a wood; down a little path, off to the right, away to the left she went, nibbling at succulent titbits she found, until . . . oh dear! She was completely and absolutely lost. Her little head looked this way and that in a panic.

'Will you allow me to show you the way home?' said a polite voice. There was Hector Hedgehog, who had noticed her leave the garden and had followed her at a distance, just in case she needed help.

He showed her home. After that, they visited each other whenever they could.

28 September
Three little ducks

Three little ducks who've strayed are we,
  Full to the brim with fun and glee!
Far from the farm where we should be,
  Three little daring ducks.

One leads the way on a big wide lake,
  One follows closely in his wake,
I am the third; what a noise I make!
  Three little noisy ducks.

Look at the sunset in the west!
  Evening is here, it's time to rest.
Up and away towards our nest!
  Three little sleepy ducks.

29 September
Bobby Robin

'Why aren't the feathers on my chest red like yours, Daddy?' asked Bobby Robin, squinting down his beak at his brown front.

'It's because you're still young,' replied his father. 'They will turn red, when you're grown up.'

But Bobby didn't want to wait until he grew up; he wanted a red breast *now*! Then he had a marvellous idea.

In the toolshed at the bottom of the garden he had noticed a tin of bright red paint. In no time at all he had flown through the open window and was happily daubing his chest with two thick layers of scarlet paint! He dropped the brush handle into the paint pot, and flew round the garden to dry himself.

Mr and Mrs Robbin nearly fell off their branch with shock! 'You look like a parrot! Wash it off at once!' chirped his mother. Luckily it was water paint, and it came off in the stream. Poor Bobby Robin!

30 September
The visitor

'Lucky! Be quiet! Come here, Lucky!' But although Tom called his dog several times, Lucky stayed where he was, jumping up and down with excitement, and barking loudly at a large hedgehog which appeared to have got stuck between the bars of the gate while trying to escape.

'Couldn't we keep it?' Tom asked wistfully. His mother, wearing a pair of thick gloves, managed to free the poor frightened creature, which then ran off.

'It lives in the woods,' she said. 'Here, Lucky would chase it.' Tom had to agree.

1 October
Training Rex

'Woof! Woof! Hello, Patsy! Where have you been?' Rex was a big, boisterous four-month-old puppy with long legs and tail, a long muzzle, and ears that pointed up when he was listening, or lay flat on his head when he was being stroked.

'I've been on holiday, and done lots of swimming,' said his neighbour, Patsy the poodle. 'You've grown a lot since I last saw you! And your bark is much stronger. What have *you* been doing?'

'I've been trying to look after my master. He's been behaving very strangely lately.' Rex looked over his shoulder to make sure he was alone, and sat down.

'Last week, he took me for a walk on a short lead. He made me walk close beside him while he kept shouting "HEEL!", and and never let me pull ahead or sniff any interesting smells which we passed. Now he does it every day! Why is that?'

Patsy thought. 'Perhaps he's frightened that an enemy will jump out at him, and wants you to protect him,' she suggested.

'Another thing he did was to pick up a stick and throw it a long way away, shouting "FETCH!" – which I didn't understand. So I sat down and looked at him. Then he took me by my collar to where he'd thrown the stick, put it in my mouth and made me bring it back. What about that?'

'My mistress likes to throw sticks for me to bring back too,' said Patsy. 'I don't understand why she does it, either; but she is very kind, so I don't mind.'

'Oh, so is my master.' Rex heard a whistle. 'That will be my dinner ready; goodbye!'

He ran off, still puzzled.

2 October
Sam the jockey

Sam was a circus dog. He had been trained to do all sorts of clever tricks, such as walking on his hind legs, jumping through a paper hoop, and riding round the ring on Jet, the black circus horse's back.

Sam loved his master and their busy life together, and was very sad when he was told one day he was too old to go on with the job. He had to retire, and a younger dog took his place.

'Never mind, old chap,' said Sam's master, 'let's go to the horse races!'

As they stood by the starting line, Sam saw a horse nearby who reminded him of Jet. He jumped up into its saddle, startling the horse, which broke loose. It joined in the race – and won it! Sam was asked to join the circus again, for one day a week!

3 October
Feeding birds

Mummy gives me a special job to do after every mealtime. When the table has been cleared, I take the cloth outside, give it a good shake, and all the crumbs are scattered around for the birds. Mummy helps me fold the cloth, and gives me any left-over food which I throw outside. Then I stand very quietly by the window and watch the birds.

The starlings are the greediest. They usually fly down in a crowd and stride about, each trying to grab the best scraps.

The robin comes along, pecking up the tiny crumbs and keeping out of the way of the bigger birds, like the pale speckled thrush and the glossy blackbird with his orange beak. *He* always sings a thank you song afterwards, from his favourite tree!

4 October
Maria's clogs

Once upon a time there lived in the forest a little girl called Maria. Her father was a woodcutter who earned very little money. They had enough to live on, but none left over for extras.

One cold winter, when the lane which Maria had to walk along to get to school was covered with ice and snow, her shoes finally wore out. Leather shoes were expensive, and the woodcutter didn't have the money to buy any.

'I'm sorry, Maria,' said her father, 'but you'll have to stay at home and help in the house until I have earned enough money to buy you another pair.'

Maria was pleased to have an excuse to stay at home. But after two or three days cooped up inside with no children to play with, she became very bored and grumpy.

Then her father had an idea. Without saying anything, he chose two pieces of beech wood, and stayed up late one night, carving, shaping and polishing, until he had made two lovely wooden clogs, with a blue daisy on the right one and a red daisy on the left! Maria was delighted.

5 October
Half' n' Half

There was once a black and white kitten who was very unhappy because of his odd colouring. You may wonder what was odd about a kitten being black and white . . . but, you see, this kitten was black from his nose as far as his middle, and white from his middle to the tip of his tail – which is very unusual!

If he was facing the mother cat, she thought he was one of her black kittens, and if he was looking the other way, she thought he was one of her white kittens! They teased him so much that he decided to leave, and find a new home.

It was cold the day he left, and after a while it started to snow. The little kitten struggled on for an hour or so, and then stopped at a doorstep, and miaowed pitifully to be let in.

A boy opened the door. 'Oh look, what a beautiful white kitten! We must rub it dry.' The poor little creature tried to hide in the towel, so they wouldn't see his real colouring; but of course they did.

'Aren't you a funny one!' smiled the boy. 'Please stay here, and we'll call you Half'n'Half!' So he did stay!

6 October
The kind frog

One year there was a drought in autumn, and instead of the usual amount of rain the sun shone for two whole weeks.

Under a hedge lay a snail, parched with thirst and too weak to crawl the short distance between it and a stream.

A small green frog hopped by. He saw the poor snail, and took pity on it.

'Climb on my back,' said the frog.

In four bounds he had reached the water's edge, and the grateful snail slipped down on to the cool, damp moss. Its life was saved.

7 October
Hard work

Anna and Paolo lived in Italy. Their house had a great many olive trees growing near it, and now the olives were ripe and ready to be picked.

'Come along, children,' said their mother, 'you are both old enough to help with the olive harvest this year. If you are good, and work hard, there will be a treat for you tonight!'

The children were each given a long stick with which they beat the branches. The olives fell on the ground and were then put into big wicker baskets.

The children worked until they were hot and tired, but they didn't want to give up before the grown-ups!

That evening, papa brought them home huge helpings of delicious ice-cream!

8 October
Morris's house

Morris Mouse decided it was time he moved house. He had spent all the summer in a corner of the old garden shed, but now the nights were getting colder he wanted to find a warmer home.

He managed to find his way up into the attic, and had a lovely time looking at all the old boxes and furniture left up there.

'What's this?' he wondered. He had found a small wooden box with a sort of dome on top, and a handle which he could push round and round. Underneath was a drawer.

'This would make an ideal house,' he squeaked happily. 'I can keep my stores under the roof, and sleep in the bedroom underneath; when I'm bored, I can have a twirl on the roundabout!'

He brought his nuts and lumps of cheese in, and then invited his friend Millie to have a ride on his roundabout.

When he went to bed that night, he found a soft mattress of grated nuts and cheese! His house was Grandma's old coffee-mill!

9 October
The lost ring

Jane took a big basket and went into the woods one day to collect hazelnuts. As she went, she threw some stale bread to the squirrels, birds and rabbits.

Suddenly she realized she had lost the new silver ring which her mother had given her for her birthday! She turned back and tried to remember which way she had come, searching all over the ground. Her little woodland friends couldn't find it either.

Then a sharp-eyed jackdaw flew down and croaked, 'What is shining in your basket?'

There amongst the nuts was Jane's ring!

10 October
Hungry Rusty!

Rusty lived in the heart of a big, leafy forest. He was a lovely rusty brown colour, with bright eyes, small pointed ears and a bushy tail, and he spent almost all his time playing in the trees. You must have guessed what he was . . . Yes, a squirrel!

All through the summer, as he grew up, he practised climbing and jumping from branch to branch, until he was the finest acrobat in the forest.

When autumn came, all the other squirrels started collecting nuts, mushrooms and acorns to store away for the winter; but Rusty didn't bother. He continued to play and show off to everyone.

Winter came, and Rusty got very hungry.

'You can share our food this time,' said his friends, 'but next year, you must use your energy to collect some for yourself!'

'I'll keep some for you!' promised Rusty.

11 October
Alex's moon flag

'Alex!' His mother was calling him.

'Alex! You're miles away; what are you dreaming about?'

'What? Oh, nothing special, Mother,' Alex answered, his mind elsewhere.

'You've always got your head in the clouds,' said his mother.

This made Alex smile, because he was just imagining what it would be like if he were an astronaut!

Ten, nine, eight, seven, six, five, four, three, two, one, BLAST OFF! Up he would rush in his rocket, until he came to land on the moon, where he would plant a flag printed with gold letters saying . . .

'Alex!' His mother called again.

'That's right, mother!' said Alex.

12 October
Three apples

Three fine, ripe apples hung on an apple tree, after all the other fruit had been picked. Now the cold October nights were here, and the apples were afraid of falling and bruising themselves.

Into the garden came Jill, holding a basket, and Daddy with a stepladder.

'Look! They're perfect; we must pick them straight away,' said Daddy, climbing up the ladder. He handed them down to Jill who put them carefully into the basket.

The apples thought they would be eaten that day, but Mummy had a better idea.

'We'll wrap them in paper, and keep them in the attic for Christmas!' she said.

The three apples felt very proud!

13 October
Nick and Brownie

It was a fine autumn day, and Nick took his little puppy Brownie for a walk in the woods.

They both caught sight of a hare in a clearing not far away. Nick stood still so as not to frighten it, but Brownie ran towards it with a friendly 'Woof! Woof! Come and play!' The hare bounded away.

Next they found a lizard sunning itself on a rock in the sunshine. Brownie wagged his tail, sniffed it – and the lizard scuttled at once between two rocks.

Nick patted the puppy, who looked quite sad. 'Never mind, Brownie; you and I will see who can find the most conkers!' They were under a horse-chestnut tree, and Nick soon had his pockets full.

Suddenly Brownie gave an excited yelp, picked something up very carefully in his mouth, and brought it over to Nick.

'That may look like a baby hedgehog,' laughed Nick, 'but it's a chestnut shell!'

14 October
The giraffe

A tall, gentle giraffe lived in a zoo, far from her native land where she had been caught when she was young. Although her keeper was kind to her, and let her walk about in a nice big enclosure with a tree in it, she couldn't help feeling lonely sometimes, and homesick for the hot climate and countryside she had been accustomed to living in.

One chilly night a monkey escaped from his cage, and found himself in the giraffe's enclosure, where she was asleep in a shelter.

'Please let me stay with you,' begged the monkey. 'Tell me about the country you and my parents came from; I was born in the zoo, so I have never seen my native land!'

The giraffe and the monkey talked long into the night, and then she found him a hollow stump where he could hide.

The giraffe never felt lonely again.

15 October
Hazelnuts

It was a cold grey day, and Corinna didn't feel like putting on a coat and going outside. Then she had an idea.

'Mummy, could we make chocolate buns with chopped nuts?' she asked eagerly. 'I haven't done any cooking for ages.'

'I'll have to see if we've got all the ingredients to make them,' said her mother, going to look in the kitchen cupboard. 'Let's see now, we need flour, sugar, margarine, chocolate powder, chopped nuts . . . oh dear! I'm afraid I've used up all the nuts, and the shops are closed today.' Poor Corinna was very disappointed, until she suddenly said, 'Wait a minute!' and dashed down the garden without waiting to put her coat on.

She was back in a few minutes with her hands full of hazelnuts. 'I remembered seeing these the other day, growing on our hazel tree!' said Corinna proudly.

She cracked open the nuts, her mother chopped them, and they baked the best chocolate buns they had ever tasted!

16 October
Winter flowers

People say there aren't any flowers in winter. But I know a secret way of having them, which I'll tell you about . . .

In the spring I find bright little violets, pale primroses and brilliant blue forget-me-nots, which I place between two sheets of paper under heavy books.

In summer, just before harvest time, I pick the scarlet poppies growing in the cornfields, and a few ears of corn.

In autumn, I find dried grasses, and pretty coloured leaves, which I press.

When winter comes, my flowers are ready to be made into pictures! That's my secret.

17 October
Blue mushrooms!

One day Sally was walking by herself in a field, when she came across the oddest mushrooms she had ever seen. There were three blue ones, in different shades, two of them spotted, and a purple one, all in a cluster near some small pink flowers.

'Whoever heard of blue mushrooms?' she murmured, picking one and staring at it.

'It must be poisonous,' she decided, and threw it as far as she could.

'How dare you! That's my best chair,' piped a little voice. She saw a tiny imp dancing up and down with rage, so she ran off to fetch the blue mushroom. When she re-planted it, the imp had disappeared!

18 October
The cricket

One day Oliver caught a cricket which he put in a box. He was thrilled with his find, and gave it grass and made plenty of small holes in the box so it could breathe.

At first it chirrupped away, but after a while it sang less and less, until Oliver became very worried and told his grandfather about it. Together, they carefully opened the box and looked at the little insect crouching low in its prison.

'The poor creature will die of boredom if you keep it shut up there any longer,' said grandfather. He looked out of the window. 'It's too cold now to put it outside; crickets like a warm dry place to spend the winter. Our hearth is very big; you could put it there, in a corner!'

Very gently, Oliver put the cricket behind a stack of wood in the hearth. When evening came and the fire burned and crackled, the cricket sang its song as gaily as when it had been in the garden!

20 October
Cyril's tail

Cyril was a very conceited grey squirrel. It was true that his fur was fine and silky, and that he probably had the longest, fluffiest tail of all the squirrels in the wood.

One day he decided his tail was long enough to hang by. He curled it round a branch, let go, and . . . slither, slip, *bump*! He landed in a pile of leaves, and took a whole hour cleaning himself up again!

19 October
The wise owl

A wise old owl
 Sat in an oak;
The more he heard
 The less he spoke.
The less he spoke
 The more he heard;
Why aren't we like
 That wise old bird?

21 October
Clever Jip!

Stephanie and Amanda were very good friends, and shared the same birthday.

This year, when the day came, Stephanie unwrapped her biggest parcel first and found a lovely pair of roller skates. She rushed outside to try them out on the concrete path, when who should arrive but Amanda, holding two new dolls and a bag of dolls' clothes.

'Just look what I've been given!' she said. 'Please come and play with these dolls! They're like you and me!'

Stephanie put the roller skates down and ran off, without noticing that one rolled as far as the dog's kennel. Jip came out, sniffed at the funny shiny thing and took it inside his kennel.

When the girls returned to try out the skates, they could only find one. After searching high and low, Stephanie called Jip, gave him one to sniff, and said, 'Go find!' How they laughed when he went into his kennel and brought out the other!

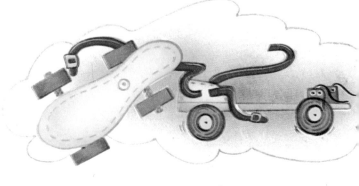

22 October
The kangaroos

Boomerang, the young kangaroo, was always up to naughty tricks. One day poor Mrs Platypus couldn't find her eggs anywhere; she went round to tell her neighbours, the kangaroo family, about her loss, and found Boomerang practising juggling with them!

His mother scolded him for his naughty behaviour, and he bounded off, laughing. Later Mrs Kangaroo met her friend Mrs Koala, who looked rather upset.

'What's the matter?' asked Mrs Kangaroo. 'Is your baby well?'

'I'm sorry to have to tell you,' said Mrs Koala, 'but your son jumped up and down under the tree Koko and I were in, and pulled such horrible faces that Koko started crying, and we had to go home.'

Poor Mrs Kangaroo was very embarrassed. She went home and told Mr Kangaroo. 'I've scolded him and told him to behave himself but it does no good,' she sighed. 'We shall lose all our friends soon.'

Mr Kangaroo thought hard. Then he called his son. 'Every morning, at seven o'clock sharp, you will have a boxing lesson.' Boomerang was delighted, and all his extra energy was used up in boxing!

23 October
The young deer

Every day, for five days, a little fawn had trotted out of the forest and come to the meadow near Tom's house, where the grass was sweet and tender. At first it was shy and nervous, but now it ran up to Tom straight away, nuzzling his hand for food, and running and playing beside him.

On the sixth day Tom managed to hitch a little cart up to the fawn, who gave him rides in it. They never noticed how late it was, until a butterfly came from Mother Deer to fetch her son home.

The fawn ran off, looking back from the forest as though to say, 'See you tomorrow!'

$$9 + 9 = 16$$

$$\begin{array}{r} 2 \\ + 2 \\ \hline 4 \end{array}$$

24 October
Late for school

The children were running about in the playground, making a noise, when the teacher blew her whistle for silence.

'Come into the classroom now, please, and I'll take the register,' she said.

They trooped in and sat down at their desks, and the teacher read out all the names in alphabetical order.

When she read out Curly's name, there was no reply.

'He's always late,' said one child. 'He's probably playing in the woods.'

Just then Curly walked in with bare feet, his hands behind his back.

'Where are your shoes, Curly?' asked the teacher, looking a little bit cross.

'I left them in the wood – but I found you some flowers!' said Curly, running up and putting them in a vase.

'Thank you,' smiled the teacher. 'We'll start off with a nature lesson today!'

25 October
Boko's new hat

Boko lived in a very hot country, where the sun at midday was right overhead.

One day Boko's mother came home from market with a new hat for him; it was made of straw, and had a fine red ribbon round it. Boko was very proud of his new hat, and ran off to show it to his friends.

'Wear it when you're playing in the sun!' called his Mummy. 'And don't lose it!'

But Boko put it on the ground while he had a game of leap-frog with a friend, and a monkey ran off with it and climbed to the top of a coconut palm! Boko couldn't climb the tree, and the monkey wouldn't come down.

Then Boko had a good idea. He and all his friends fetched saucepans and spoons from home, stood under the tree, and then banged as hard as they could! The monkey dropped the hat, and Boko put it on!

26 October
Flop-Ears' treat

Flop-Ears, the young rabbit, was very bored. He had been in hospital for a week with a rash and a temperature, and although he was much better now, he still didn't feel like eating much.

The kind nurse tried to help him with his lunch. 'Come along now, Flop-Ears, you'll never get strong if you don't eat up your food! Here's a spoonful for Mummy, one for Daddy, one for all your friends in the hospital, and one for me!' It was vegetable soup for lunch that day, which was not Flop-Ears' favourite.

Daddy came to visit him in the afternoon with a bag of scrubbed baby carrots, radishes and fresh lettuce leaves – all things that Flop-Ears loved. 'You're coming home tomorrow!' said Daddy.

Later Flop-Ears went round the ward giving a carrot or a radish to all his friends. He would have more at home!

27 October
The race

Cosmo was the farm donkey. He worked hard, sometimes carrying loads on his back, and sometimes pulling the donkey cart out to the fields and back, and round the farm.

Polo was a sleek, brown colt. He was much bigger than Cosmo, and took the big cart to market twice a week in the busy town not far away. The farmer's children, Dick and Dorothy, liked to go to market too. They brushed Polo's coat until it shone, polished his hooves, and took all the tangles out of his mane and tail.

'We can't let you go to town with mud on your coat,' said Dick. 'It doesn't matter about Cosmo, because he never goes outside the farm.' Polo tossed his head proudly and neighed to Cosmo, who was standing watching with his coat all muddy and matted in the next field.

The children took it in turns to ride Polo round his field from time to time. One day, Dick said to Dorothy, 'Let's have a race! You're smaller, so you ride Cosmo, and we'll race to the river!'

'I don't want to ride a muddy donkey,' grumbled Dorothy; but she agreed.

Away they went! Polo started to show off and canter, and Dick soon fell off. Cosmo trotted steadily all the way, and won!

'Well done, Cosmo!' said Dorothy. 'I'll brush you, and ride you to market!'

28 October
Rain

Where's the sun? Here comes the rain,
  Beating on the window pane.
In my boots and mackintosh
  I can jump and make a SPLOSH!

Cats hate rain, and so do dogs,
  Not like snails and fish and frogs.
As for ducks, they think it's fun;
  They're not waiting for the sun!

29 October
In the evening

It's evening now at the farm, and the animals will soon be asleep for the night.

The farmer's wife is in the shed, milking the last cow, while it stands quietly chewing hay.

The horse has finished its evening feed of oats, and stands with drooping head and eyes half closed, tired after its busy day pulling the cart round the farm.

In the pig-sty, you can hear some grunting and squeaking going on; are the piglets squabbling again?

The farmer's little girl is throwing handfuls of grain to the cock and his hens. It's her job to feed them every night and then shut them up safely, in case the fox is on the prowl.

'Woof! Woof! Don't forget me!' barks Shep; and Puss laps her bedtime drink of milk.

30 October
The picture

I was so bored yesterday afternoon! It was raining, I had no one to play with, I had read all my books and I couldn't think of anything nice to do. So I went to ask Mummy for a good idea.

'Wait here!' she said, and went up to her room. In a minute she was down again, with a packet of different coloured sheets of paper, glue, scissors and a big tray.

'See if you can cut out shapes and make a lovely bright picture,' she said. She gave me a big sheet of white paper.

First I cut out a big blue square for a house, then little yellow squares for lighted windows. Then I made a big red triangle for the roof. I nearly forgot the door! That was red too.

Next came some brown tree trunks, with plenty of green leaves stuck on them. I made a blue bird, and sat it in a brown nest in one of the trees! After that, I cut out lots of flowers, in pink, red, yellow and blue, and made a garden.

I gave the picture to Mummy.

I'll make one for Daddy when it rains another time!

31 October
Animal quiz

'Let's have an animal quiz!' said Uncle Peter, who was in charge of his two nieces and little nephew, Billy, for the day.

'What's a quiz?' asked Billy, who was only three years old.

'Do you two girls know?' asked their uncle; but they both shook their heads.

'A quiz is a game with questions and answers. I'm going to ask the questions, and you three will give me the answers. I shall ask you one at a time, and there's to be no interrupting, please! Someone keep the score on a piece of paper, and at the end we'll see how many points each person has.'

Judy, who was nearly seven, wrote their three names at the top of a sheet of paper and drew lines down for columns.

'I'll start with Billy: which animal is very big, grey, with a long nose which it uses for sucking up water?'

'An elephant,' answered Billy at once.

'Very good; one point to Billy. Pam, do you know a very tall animal with a long neck, and long legs?'

'Easy!' said Pam. 'A giraffe.'

'A point to Pam,' said Uncle Peter. 'Write it down, Judy! Now a harder one: what is the huge creature that swims in the sea like a fish, but isn't a fish?'

'That's not hard! It's a whale,' laughed Judy, giving herself a point.

'Now for the second round; Billy, what animal has its coat cut off each year?'

'A poodle,' said Billy, and looked very surprised when his sisters laughed. 'Fifi does,' he said, patting their poodle.

'You're right; and there's another animal, whose coat is used to make into clothes and other things.'

'Oh! A sheep, of course,' said Billy.

'Pam, can you give me a bird that runs fast, but cannot fly?'

Pam thought. 'An ostrich,' she said.

'Judy, a bird that swims, but can't fly?'

'Wait a minute . . . a penguin,' she said. 'We all have two points, let's go on!'

The animal quiz lasted all morning!

1 November
The pancakes

Every year in the Blue Kingdom each family in the land made a present for Prince John's birthday. It was the custom to bake a special dish from home-grown food, and as everyone was very fond of their prince, there were some delicious presents.

One year Sylvia's family found that nothing was growing in their garden. Sylvia's mother did not know how she would find a birthday present for the prince, so she sent Sylvia to seek the advice of her godmother, the Blue Fairy.

'Carry this basket home carefully,' said the fairy. 'Don't uncover it until it is safely on your kitchen table!'

Sylvia did as she was told. When she and her mother unpacked the basket, they found eggs, flour, milk and a pot of jam.

'There's not enough flour there to make a cake,' said Sylvia's mother. However, they mixed it carefully with the eggs and milk, saving the jam for later. They poured a little of the runny mixture into a frying pan, turned it, rolled some jam up in it, and ate half each.

'It's delicious!' smiled Sylvia. 'Let's call them pancakes, and give some to Prince John! I'm sure he'd like them.'

Of course, he liked them very much!

2 November
The new lodger

Out in the road one day a tiny flea felt the cold wind blowing, and noticed how it blew the dead leaves about.

'Winter's nearly here,' she said to herself. 'I must find a safe home soon.'

At that very moment, along came a big dog with a good thick coat.

'That's the place for me!' thought the flea, and with one great bound landed on the dog's head. But Spot, the dog, felt the flea, and quickly shook it off.

The little flea was not going to be put off so easily; she hopped on to Spot's nose and spoke politely to him. 'Please, Mr Dog, let me shelter in your warm fur from the cold wind,' she pleaded. 'I haven't any fur of my own, and I feel the cold terribly.'

Spot was a kind dog. 'All right then, you can stay, as long as you don't tickle me,' he agreed. 'If I start scratching, my master will sprinkle special powder all over me and that will be the end of you!'

The flea thanked Spot and promised to be good. I wonder if she kept her promise!

3 November
Little Fox Cub

Little Fox Cub was daydreaming again . . .

An aeroplane flew by in the distance, shiny and huge. 'That's what I'd really like to be – an airline pilot with a lot of buttons to press and knobs to turn and levers to pull.' He ran off to ask his father if he could train as a pilot.

Mr Fox went to discuss the matter with the other woodland creatures. They all came to the same conclusion: impossible!

'Give him a good reason, or he might run off and try!' warned Mr Owl.

'If you went to train as a pilot, the men might never let you go,' his father told him next day. 'Anyway, you're not tall enough to see where you're going, through the windscreen; and aeroplanes are noisy, smelly things.'

Little Fox Cub sighed. 'I'd better stay,' he said, gazing up at another aeroplane.

4 November
Up in the attic

It was Sunday afternoon, it was raining, and the twins were bored.

'I'm going up into the attic to do some tidying,' said their mother briskly. 'Who wants to help?'

'I do,' said Tina quickly.

'So do I,' said Tania, never wanting to be left out.

'Fetch your aprons then, and I'll give you a broom and a duster. You can take it in turns to sweep and dust. There'll be plenty of cobwebs up there!'

They ran up the rough wooden staircase and as soon as they stepped inside the dusty room, full of old things, the twins forgot the real reason for their visit!

'Oh look, Tania! Here's my old doll – the one that lost an eye. She's dirty, poor thing! Let's give her a bath!'

'Tina! Look at this beautiful silk dress! I wonder who it belonged to.'

'I wore it as a bridesmaid when I was your age,' said Mummy. She smiled, and said nothing about the work they said they would do. They played up their quite happily for the rest of the afternoon.

5 November
Hungry bluetits

In the abandoned garden the flowers and shrubs had been left untouched all the summer. The grass and weeds grew waist high, and of course it was a wonderful place for birds and little animals to make their nests, undisturbed by men with their sharp cutting tools, and rakes.

The bluetits had chosen an old apple tree to build their nest in. It seemed such a good place, they had decided to have a second family later in the summer, and there was still a young bird left in the nest. The frosts had come early that year, killing the insects they liked to eat; what could the parents do to feed their young one?

A cold wind shook the branches of the apple tree, sending some fruit thudding down into the neighbours' garden. The old lady who lived there looked up into the tree and saw the young bluetit in its nest, with a hungry open beak. Straight away, she fetched scraps and left them on a table. Soon, the little bird learned to fly, and find its own food.

6 November
Cold feet!

The sun had shone brightly all day, but when dusk fell a cold mist had formed, chilling the air and making it damp.

Nancy was curled up in bed, covered with a sheet, three blankets and a large eiderdown, trying to get her feet warm. She rubbed them, turned them round and round in circles, wriggled her toes – but it was no good; they were still cold.

'Mummy!' she called. 'My feet are freezing!'

'I'll bring you something unusual,' said Mummy. Something unusual? Whatever could that be!

In a few minutes, Mummy came in with a long-handled copper pan, like a frying pan with a hinged lid.

'What's that?' laughed Nancy.

'It's a warming pan,' explained her mother. 'I've kept it in the loft for years. In the old days, Granny used to put glowing charcoal in it, and put it in her bed to make it warm. I'm cooking supper on the charcoal grill tonight, so we can use the warming pan for your bed, if you like!'

'Oh yes, Mummy! I'd like it every time you use charcoal,' said Nancy happily.

7 November
Grandfather

Grandfather lived in a tiny flat at the top of the house where Marion and her parents lived. He was old and didn't talk much, and spent a lot of time sitting in his leather armchair, reading books. She hardly ever saw him.

One day Marion heard that Grandfather had a sore foot. She felt sorry for him, and decided to take him a rose from the garden. She tapped nervously on his door.

'Come in,' he said, and Marion walked in and gave him the rose, too shy to speak.

He smiled. 'What a lovely present! Thank you very much. Would you like a biscuit? And do you like chocolate mousse?' Before she could answer, he had got up, and gone to fetch a tin of delicious biscuits and a large helping of her favourite pudding. Soon, she was telling him all about what she was doing at school.

'I could help you with your reading tomorrow, if you like,' said Grandfather. 'Now, here's a little present for *you*.' He gave her a glass paper-weight with a castle inside, and when she shook it a snow storm appeared.

'Oh, thank you Grandfather! I'll come tomorrow,' she said, and ran downstairs.

8 November
Goldie

Goldie was a marmalade cat with a white front and round green eyes. He had been born in the spring, and this was his first autumn. He couldn't understand what was happening to the trees, which of course were losing their leaves.

All through the summer, he used to spend many hours hiding in a fork of the willow tree, screened by the curtain of pale leaves which hung to the ground, watching the birds and always hoping to catch one – although he never succeeded! And the tall grasses, where he had crouched and stalked fieldmice, again without much success – they had all died down, or been cut and tidied away.

The trouble with Goldie was that he was lazy, and spoiled by his mistress, Kathy. He only pretended to hunt for his food.

'Come on, Goldie! Dinner's ready!' He ran inside for his usual bowl of cat-food.

9 November
The lonely owl

Olive, the owl, was very unhappy. She knew she had an important job to do, perching on the branch of a tree each night and standing guard for the birds who slept in the tree; but it was such a boring job! She hardly ever saw anyone to chat to – just the occasional fox or badger, and perhaps another owl to exchange hoots with, and that was all.

What could she do to change her life for the better? Poor Olive couldn't stand bright light, so when the sun rose in the morning, wakening the day birds, she went to sleep in her nest in the hollow tree.

One fine night, as she sat hunched glumly on a branch, racking her brains for a good idea, she had one!

'I'll wear sun glasses!' she decided.

When the birds work next morning, they were amazed to be greeted by a friendly lady owl wearing dark glasses!

11 November
Carlo the barber

It was afternoon at the zoo, and Carlo the coyote was going for a stroll, looking for someone to talk to or something to do.

Suddenly he noticed a pair of shears left on the path by a careless gardner.

'Aha!' he chuckled. 'Now I can have some fun,' and he looked around.

Brutus, the lion, was having his afternoon siesta. While he lay snoring, Carlo cut all round Brutus's long thick mane. Then, worried that he might have got himself into bad trouble, he ran and hid.

Brutus was surprised to find his mane short when he woke, and soon found Carlo.

'Thank you!' he roared. 'I'm much more comfortable now. You're a good barber, Carlo!' The coyote was very relieved.

10 November
Grumpy rabbit

There was once a very difficult young rabbit who was always discontented.

When he was at home, he was bored. When his mother took him out in the field to play, he always seemed to prick his paws on thistles.

When he sat down to a special lunch of fresh carrots, he said he didn't feel like eating carrots that day . . . and when the table was cleared he said he was still hungry!

When it was bedtime he wanted to stay up, and when it was time to get up in the morning he wanted to stay in bed.

Poor mother and father rabbit didn't know what to do with their difficult son.

Then Mr Hedgehog gave him an accordion and taught him some tunes. 'If you want to complain, play a tune instead,' he said.

That rabbit never grumbled again, and now he plays the accordion very well!

12 November
Going sliding

'Come on Dandy! Come and slide on the ice with us,' shouted the two rabbit brothers to their friend, the fawn.

'I'll watch how you do it first,' said Dandy, trotting up to the edge of the frozen lake.

The rabbits took a run down the snowy bank of the lake and then jumped on to the ice, crouching low over their paws, as they slid straight across.

'It's easy!' they shouted. 'Your turn now, Dandy!'

The little deer ran down the bank and took a mighty spring into the air. He landed so fast on his shiny little hooves and spindly legs, that his feet shot away from under him, and he arrived the other side lying on his back with his feet waving in the air!

'I seem to be better at jumping than sliding,' he laughed. 'Show me again!'

13 November
A narrow squeak

Looking very smart in her black and white feathers, Margot the magpie crossed the garden with cautious, dainty hops.

Her round bright eyes glanced nervously from side to side, making sure no one was about.

Fluff, the rabbit, was busy nibbling a carrot under the hedge; he was a friend, so that was all right.

Margot eyed the dog kennel suspiciously and listened, her head on one side. Quiet snoring coming from inside told her that Lucifer, the dog, was asleep. As for her worst enemy, Kooky the cat, Margot had just seen her hunting for fieldmice in the long grass.

Now Margot had her eye on the three pets' food bowls; she hopped closer and closer, and took a quick peck from each in turn. Mm! The cat food tasted best. Throwing caution to the winds, she tucked in to Kooky's dinner . . .

SQUAWK! Flutter and *pounce*! Kooky had returned, and nearly caught Margot, who flew into a tree. What a narrow squeak!

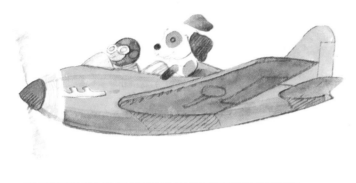

14 November
The flying dog

Patch's master had his own small aeroplane, which he flew most weekends. If he was just going for a short flight, he took Patch with him to the aerodrome, and left him to run about and look at the planes on the ground. Patch was very well behaved and the other pilots let him jump inside their planes sometimes and pretend to go for a ride in them.

Patch longed to fly in his master's aeroplane, but his master thought flying was too dangerous for a dog.

One day Patch was at the aerodrome while his master was chatting to the man in the control tower. Patch saw his chance, and ran quickly over to the plane, jumped in, and hid himself away in the back.

VROOM! VROOM! In a few moments the engine started up, the plane turned and sped down the runway, and then . . . up and away they went! What an exciting feeling, being up in the air at last!

Patch sat up for a moment, but the wind blew past him so strongly he was afraid it would blow his ears off, so he got under the seat again until they landed.

His master was amazed to see him jump out. 'Brave dog!' he said, patting him.

15 November
A winter legend

Many, many years ago, a fairy wanted to make a white dress for a moonlit ball.

But it was late autumn, and the earth was covered with shades of gold, russet and brown. Where could she find something of pure white to make into a ball gown?

Then she had an idea. She carried some eiderdowns from the fairy queen's palace up on to the roof, and took out all the feathers. Then she blew her magic whistle to summon the cold north wind. It came at once, blowing the feathers in swirling clouds down on to the earth below, where they became pure white snow flakes. Then she emptied a sack of diamond dust, and summoned the east wind, who came and blew it all over the snow, turning it into sparkling frost. The fairy made her dress – and every winter the cold winds bring us snow and glittering frost.

16 November
The new red slippers

A pair of beautiful red slippers, which had never been worn, were lying in a box at the back of a wardrobe. They were very proud of their smart appearance and fluffy red pom-poms.

The slippers often had visits from other shoes, because the wardrobe was in a boy's bedroom, and the boy often had to change his shoes. But the slippers were too grand to talk to any of them.

One day the door was opened and an old grey slipper was thrown in beside them. It was worn out and full of holes.

'Don't come near us!' said the red slippers. 'You're so dirty and ugly!'

'It's your turn now to be worn and scuffed and rubbed!' grinned the grey slipper. 'You'll look like me in a year!'

17 November
A secret lodger

A lodger has come to live in our house, and I am the only person who knows about him. If you can keep a secret, I'll tell you how I found out . . .

A few nights ago I crept into the kitchen for a glass of milk. I opened the door quietly so as not to disturb anyone, and saw a little brown mouse on the floor by the fridge. He ran off at once, and wriggled through a small hole in the wall.

I could see he was thin, so I took a small piece of cheese and put it on the floor by his hole. Soon I saw a twitching nose, followed by whiskers and a pair of bright eyes. He came out, ate up the cheese, and ran back into his hole again.

Now I come down every evening and feed him. *Please* don't tell anyone, will you?

18 November
The fire chief

Sebastian had been given a magnificent toy fire engine – not an ordinary small one, but a big shiny red one with a key to wind it up and make it go, long extending ladders and a hose that really worked. Sebastian was the chief fire officer, and was called out to fight fires in all the different rooms of the house at least twenty times in the afternoon.

'Ting-a-ling! Ting-a-ling! Out of the way, everyone!' he shouted, rushing into the kitchen to put out another raging fire.

'Would the chief fire officer be able to take time off for tea?' enquired Mummy. He agreed, but kept the fire engine close by him – just in case!

19 November
The champion footballers

One Saturday Peter and his new friend, Luke, decided to take a football on to the common and practise kicking goals.

'I usually play forward in school games,' said Peter, 'so don't be surprised if I get more goals than you.'

'Well, I'm often goalkeeper,' grinned Luke, 'so we'll see about that!'

They found a place where there was no one too near, and stuck two poles into the ground for goalposts.

'Let's have five shots each,' said Peter. 'You be goalkeeper first!'

Peter took the ball back some distance, put it down, took a run and WHAM! kicked it straight towards the middle of the goal. Luke saved it easily, and threw it back. 'You'll have to do better than that,' he said. 'You've got four more shots now!'

After that, Peter aimed at the corners of the goal, getting all four shots in.

Then it was Luke's turn to shoot. He dribbled the ball close to the goal, and when he shot, Peter couldn't get near it! He got the next three shots in too, but the last missed. The score was four all!

'We are the champions!' they both sang, as they ran home together afterwards.

20 November
Granny Florence

My three brothers and I have a very special friend. She is an old lady, who lives all alone except for her white cat, Minerva, in a little cottage at the end of the lane. We call her Granny Florence.

When the weather is cold, we do jobs for her, like shopping, tidying her garden, and fetching logs for the fire. Afterwards she invites us in, and gives us sweets or chocolates, and roast chestnuts.

Granny Florence sits in front of the fire, with Minerva on her knee, waiting for her soup to cook, while we gather round, hoping for a story.

'Long ago, when I was a girl,' she starts, and we listen, fascinated, to stories of her childhood over sixty years ago.

21 November
The twins

Tom and Tim were identical twins. In other words they looked exactly like each other – so much so that even their own parents had difficulty in telling them apart. They were wicked little rascals, too, and got away with all sorts of naughty tricks, each saying it was the other who had done it.

One day, Tim found an enormous strawberry flan in the larder. He cut himself a slice and ate it, then another – and soon half the flan had disappeared! Tom came to look for him, and ate up the rest!

When their mother came to get lunch ready, she was very annoyed indeed to find the flan had gone. She called through the kitchen window to Tim, who was kicking his football. 'Did you eat up the flan?'

'Oh no, Mother; have you asked Tom?'

She found Tom reading. 'Did you eat the flan, Tom?' she asked, but he said no, too.

When they were called to lunch, they said they couldn't eat any, so their mother knew they had lied. 'You may not play together again today,' she said.

22 November
The burglary

One frosty evening Pipkin the squirrel came home to find that his house had been burgled, and all his precious provisions, which he had worked so hard to collect, had been stolen.

Pipkin started to cry. 'What will become of me?' he sobbed. 'It's hard enough to find food when the ground is hard and frosty, but when the snow falls there'll be nothing at all for me to eat, and I shall starve. Oh dear, what shall I do?'

Hearing all the noise, a kind owl woke and flew over to Pipkin. 'Don't despair,' she told him. 'Do you see that house over there? They put seeds, bread, and all sorts of titbits out for the birds every day, and there should be some for you too.'

When the little girl who lived there saw Pipkin coming, she put nuts out on the window sill, and they became good friends.

23 November
Cyclone's tricks

Jeremy could hear the circus music faintly in the distance, as he left his house and ran off down the road in the direction of the village green. He had been at school when the circus had arrived and he couldn't wait to go and have a look around while the afternoon performance was on.

As he ran past one of Farmer Brown's fields, he saw an extraordinary sight. For some months a beautiful white horse had been kept in the field. It was quiet and well behaved, and always trotted up when Jeremy walked past, hoping for a friendly pat, and perhaps some food. But today, it was standing up on its hind legs, waving its forelegs in the air while it turned round!

Jeremy stopped and watched, amazed. 'You clever horse!' he said. It heard him, and trotted over, tossing its head and whinnying excitedly. Jeremy gave it a lump of sugar, and the horse started to prance round the field at a slow trot, lifting its feet high in the air.

'I must tell Farmer Brown about this,' Jeremy decided, and ran off to the farm.

Farmer Brown smiled when Jeremy told him what the horse was doing. 'Cyclone used to be a circus horse,' he explained. 'I bought him when he was too old to perform!'

'He heard the music and remembered his tricks,' smiled Jeremy. 'I must give him an apple for being so clever.' He ran off, hoping Cyclone would do some more tricks.

24 November
Roast chestnuts

It's nearly dark, the fire burns bright,
   What shall we do this wintry night?
Let's fetch the pan that's full of holes,
   And roast some chestnuts on the coals!
They are delicious things to eat,
   We all agree; oh, what a treat!

25 November
Cleo's hat

Cleo was a very timid young marmot lady.
When young gentlemen marmots came to
invite her to go for a walk, she was too shy
to answer, so they went away again.

'She'll never marry,' said her friends.

There was going to be a ball one night,
and the ladies sometimes wore hats to these
occasions.

'I haven't a hat, so I can't go,' said Cleo,
who didn't want to go to the ball, and was
using the hat as an excuse.

But on the morning of the ball, some of
her friends brought her a beautifully
decorated straw hat, covered with flowers,
leaves and berries, which they had made
specially for her; so she had to go!

On the way to the ball, the hat blew
off Cleo's head, and was spoiled. Poor Cleo
burst into tears; it had been *such* a
beautiful hat!

'Dry your eyes, Cleo! You look pretty
without a hat,' said a handsome marmot,
offering her his arm. She lost her hat, but
she found a husband that evening!

26 November
Make-believe

After Mummy has said goodnight, and just
before I fall asleep, I like to imagine that
I am someone quite different.

Last night I was Tarzan. I had a lion as
my pet, whom I had rescued from a trap
when he was a cub, and who let me ride
him through the jungle, protecting me
from all danger. He slept at my feet in the
cave where I lived and roared very loudly
at everyone else, but never at me.

'Goodnight, Mummy!' Click! Out goes
the light; who shall I be tonight?

I know . . . I'm an underwater explorer,
looking for treasure in a ship that sank
hundreds of years ago. What is shining
down there . . . gold? The sun is in my eyes,
it's morning, and I've been dreaming!

27 November
Old photographs

'Oh no! Not raining again,' groaned Anna.

'It rained last Sunday, and it's raining again this Sunday,' grumbled her younger sister, Karen; just when I wanted to take Beano for a walk in the park.'

'Beano doesn't seem to mind,' their mother smiled, seeing the dog asleep in front of the fire. 'Let me see if I can find something interesting to show you . . .'

She disappeared for a minute, and came back with a thick, heavy album tucked under her arm. 'This photograph album is nearly a hundred years old,' she said.

The girls sat up to the table and gently turned the first page. 'Look! All the ladies are wearing long dresses, and big funny hats,' laughed Karen. 'Isn't that our park they're walking in?'

'It was their park then,' Mummy smiled.

'This lady has a big lump at the back of her dress,' said Anna.

'That is your great-great-grandmother, and she is wearing a bustle,' said Mummy. 'They were considered elegant, then.' She left the girls, saying 'Your clothes will look quaint in a hundred years.'

'I hadn't thought of that,' Anna smiled.

28 November
A cosy nest

Pippa flew to and fro under the cold, cloudy sky, chirping and twittering plaintively. 'Oh dear, oh dear! What shall I do? What shall I do?'

'Why are you still here?' chirrupped Nellie, the nightingale. 'All the other swallows left for Africa long ago.'

Pippa flew down on to the branch beside Nellie, trying to fluff out her sleek feathers as the other birds did, to keep out the chilling wind.

'I didn't feel like flying all that distance,' she grumbled. 'Anyway, with so many kind friends here, surely there's *one* who will help me?' She looked hopefully at Nellie.

'Very well then; come and warm up in my nest, while we think of a good place for you to stay all winter,' said Nellie kindly. Pippa snuggled down gratefully.

'Look! Mr Thomas always leaves his loft window open a crack,' chirped Nellie. 'You could stay there.' Wasn't Pippa lucky?

29 November
James's visitor

James had to stay in bed because he had a bad cold and earache. He was not allowed visitors. His mother was worried because he wouldn't eat his food, and he wouldn't drink his medicine.

Suddenly she remembered the little lady in the musical box. Weeks ago she had seen a wooden painted box in the shape of a cottage with a key sticking out of it, in a shop window. It was a musical box.

'I'll buy it, and give it to James on some special occasion,' she decided, and put it away in a secret drawer.

'The right time has arrived,' she thought to herself, and fetched the musical box. 'There's a tiny visitor in here, waiting to see you when you've had your medicine,' she told him. He sat up and gulped it down. 'Now, turn the key five times, and press the chimney down.'

James did so, and a gay little tune tinkled away, while a tiny painted wooden lady came out, turned and went in again.

James had no more trouble with medicine!

30 November
Happy Harriet

Doctors tell us that people can catch colds from each other, and that nasty illnesses like measles and chickenpox are also catching. In Harriet's case it seemed to be her smile that was catching!

If she heard the milkman in the road before she went to school, she would run out with a basket to save him walking up the path. His rather grumpy face would light up with a smile when he saw Harriet's happy little face.

If the weather was cold, or it rained, Harriet kept herself cheerful on her walk to and from school by skipping along, or humming a gay little tune. She smiled at anyone who looked cold or miserable, and they smiled back! Even the babies crying in their prams stopped at once, and started gurgling happily when Harriet stayed for a moment and played with them.

Every Saturday she went to visit her grandmother, and always took a bunch of flowers from the garden. Now there were none, but she found some leaves and berries which she made into a pretty arrangement.

'What a lovely posy!' Granny smiled.

1 December
The legend of the pine tree

The fairy of the forest was getting very annoyed with her subjects, the trees. They were all quarrelling amongst themselves as to which had the best leaves.

'Mine are the biggest,' boasted the chestnut.

'Mine give the deepest shade,' said the oak.

'Mine are the most beautiful colour,' insisted the copper beech, and so on. They laughed at the little pine, and said it wasn't a real tree at all as it had needles instead of leaves.

The forest fairy turned herself into a squirrel, and asked each tree in turn if she could build her nest in their topmost branches. Each one refused, except for the pine, which welcomed her. She climbed to the top, changed back into a fairy, and punished the other trees by making them lose all their leaves in winter.

That is why the tall, evergreen pine tree becomes king of the forest, and why we have one in our homes at Christmas – often with a little fairy on the top!

216

2 December
Journeys

'It's time we got the globe out and played the journey game,' said Daddy one day.

'Hooray!' shouted John. He loved going on journeys round the globe.

Daddy put the globe on the table, and showed them where they lived.

'We shall all go on our first trip together,' said Daddy, 'to a country which is very hot and dry, with big deserts. There are strange buildings called pyramids . . .'

'Egypt!' shouted John, and they all found it on the globe.

'Now it's my turn! I'm going to a place where the people speak French and like eating snails. In the capital city is a tall tower which you can climb . . .'

'That's in Paris, and the country is France,' said Claire. 'We went there!'

3 December
Marbles

Fiona and Gordon decided it was a long time since they had played marbles.

'I hope we still have enough to play with,' said Fiona. 'I'm afraid some may be lost.'

They looked in their odds and ends box, and found five red marbles, two yellow and two green.

'Oh dear,' said Gordon. 'We can't have a good game unless we have five each of one colour. Let's ask Mummy for some money to go and buy some more.'

Gordon asked his mother, but she said they should first look in every cupboard and corner of their bedrooms. Fiona found another yellow one under her bed.

'You can go and buy two yellow ones,' said their mother.

'Please Mummy, could we buy three green as well?' Then three people could play!'

Her mother laughed, and gave them the money. 'All right! You win,' she said.

4 December
Roller skates

Simon had saved up all his pocket money, and bought himself a pair of roller skates. Now it seemed to his father he spent every minute of his free time outside, skating.

'That boy should read more,' he grumbled to Simon's mother, 'or play football.'

'I expect it's just a craze,' she said. 'He wants to be the best skater at school.'

One day, Simon's father telephoned from the station on his way to work. 'I've left my wallet at home with all my money in it, and the train leaves in ten minutes!' he said.

'Give it to me! I'll go on roller skates,' said Simon, and got there just in time.

His father was very impressed. 'I must buy some!' he said, and they both laughed.

5 December
The party

Hey diddle diddle!
   Just look at that fiddle!
He's laughing and jumping about.
   The little drum's prancing,
He's so good at dancing
   And waving his drumsticks about!

The trumpet looks worried,
   He's dizzy and flurried,
He can't dance as well as the rest.
   The lady guitar
Is the smartest by far;
   Her clothes and her hat are the best.

The party is humming;
   But who is this coming?
Look out! The conductor is near . . .
   The instruments race
To get back into place.
   That's the end of the party, I fear!

6 December
Saint Nicholas

'Mummy, my friend Kirsten at school told me that in her country today is Saint Nicholas Day. Who is he?' asked Dinah.

'He was a bishop who lived in a place called Anatolia, a long time ago. They say that he performed a miracle and brought three dead children back to life. That is why he became the patron saint of children. Now they say that every year, on his special day, he rides through the countries of the north on a donkey, and gives sweets and toys to all the children.'

'I wish we lived in one of those places,' said Dinah wistfully, 'then we could have presents today too! It isn't fair.'

Mummy laughed. 'Didn't you know? *Their* Saint Nicholas is *our* Santa Claus, and he'll bring you presents too! Just wait a little longer, that's all. After all, he has a long journey to make . . .'

7 December
Making presents

Jane wrote in large letters on a piece of paper DO NOT DISTURB! and hung it on her bedroom doorknob. Then she fetched a big box containing coloured paper, cardboard, beads, shells which she had collected last summer and glue, and put it on the table. She was going to make presents.

'I'll make a frame for Mummy,' she decided. 'I can stick these pretty yellow shells all round the edge of this blue piece of cardboard; and I'll make a cut out collage picture for Daddy.'

Jane heard the door push open, and tried to cover everything with her arms . . . but it was only Tigger the cat, who couldn't read. Curious as usual, he jumped on the table, scattering shells everywhere.

'You don't deserve a present,' she sighed.

8 December
The reindeer

Grandfather had been telling Kipi, the little boy from Lapland, another story about the great white magic reindeer.

'I'm going to find out whether this is a real animal, or whether Grandfather has been making up stories,' Kipi said to himself. 'If I see it, and kill it, I'll know it's real.' He put on his warm clothes and boots, fastened on his skis, and went off with his bow and arrow.

When he had gone some distance, he saw the giant form of a white reindeer silhouetted against the sky, with immense sparkling horns and flashing eyes.

'Do not kill me,' it said, 'and you will have good luck all your life.'

Kipi turned round and went home on his skis as fast as he could to tell Grandfather about it.

9 December
So many toys!

Joy had been taken to the toy department of a big store by her aunt. There were so many lovely toys there that Joy wanted to play with, so when her aunt's back was turned she jumped inside an empty packing case and hid. Soon, the store had closed!

Without a thought for her poor worried aunt, Joy jumped out of the box, and started playing with all the toys!

'Come on, dolls, you must all get undressed and have a bath! Then you can put on party dresses, I'll brush your hair, and we'll invite all these teddies to tea! We'll need lots of china tea-sets for so many dolls, and some pretend food . . .'

Two hours later, the night watchman was amazed to find her asleep in a Wendy house, hugging eight dolls and ten teddy-bears!

10 December
The snow queen

Sally and Laura were making up stories.

'When I'm grown up, I shall be the Queen of the Snow,' said Sally.

'How will you do that?' asked Laura, not believing her.

'I shall marry the King of the Ice, and live in a beautiful castle built of crystals and diamonds. I shall wear a shining white dress and a fluffy cloak made of snowflakes, and I shall drive across my kingdom in a sledge covered in precious stones pulled by a white reindeer with golden bells on its harness, and I shall hang icicles in the trees.'

'Pooh!' said Laura. 'In a cold place like that, your nose would go red!'

'No it wouldn't!' said Sally indignantly. 'And if you were rude to me, I'd turn you into a block of ice!'

'I'm going to marry the Prince of Summer, and we'll come and melt all your ice and snow into water,' said Laura.

Both the girls burst out laughing!

11 December
Barnaby and the wolf cub

Barnaby lived on the edge of the great forests of northern Canada.

One day he set off on his sledge, drawn by two huskies, to find a suitable pine tree for Christmas. He had left the sledge, and was walking about looking for a neat bushy pine, when he heard some plaintive whimpering, and saw a young wolf cub lying wounded by an oak tree. Its mother lay dead, shot by a huntsman.

Barnaby gave up his search for a tree, picked the cub up gently, and tucked it up on the sledge, under the fur rug. He drove home quickly, and his father removed a bullet from the cub's shoulder.

With Barnaby's loving care and attention the wolf cub recovered, and the two became great friends. When it was old enough to fend for itself, Barnaby encouraged it to go and live in the forest, which it did. But the wolf never forgot Barnaby and his kindness.

12 December
Granny's knitting

When Betty and Paul were invited to tea with their grandmother, they decided to ask her to knit them something each.

'Please Granny, will you knit me a red jersey?' begged Betty.

'And will you knit me a pair of purple socks?' Paul asked eagerly.

Granny laughed. 'I can't finish both presents by Christmas, but I might manage the socks,' she said.

Next day, she had invited two friends in to tea, and she knitted away at the first sock while they all chatted together.

'Thank you for the delicious tea!' they said as they left; Granny looked at the sock and found it was at least three times as long as Paul's leg! Then she had an idea . . . When the children next came, they saw a long, purple sausage-dog, lying against the door, keeping the draught out!

13 December
Marina's find

Marina had not yet arrived at school.

'Well, we'll just have to start our lesson without her,' said her teacher.

Scrape, scrape, scrape. All heads turned to the door at the sound of someone cleaning the snow off their boots.

Knock, knock! 'Come in, Marina!' called the teacher.

The little girl walked into the room holding something small, wrapped up in the loose ends of her scarf. 'I'm sorry I'm late,' she said, her face red from embarrassment and cold, 'But I couldn't leave the poor little thing, could I? He's half frozen – look!'

All the children gathered round at once, exclaiming. 'What is it? It's a bird. Is it alive? It looks like a sparrow!'

They made it a nest in a box by the radiator, and by midday it was well again!

14 December
Little angel

There was once a little angel who lived in a picture frame above a fireplace. She looked very sweet and innocent; but often she was thinking about the tricks she might play when her birthday came round. Once a year, she was allowed to fly out of her picture frame and amuse herself for the whole of her birthday.

If the family she lived with forgot her birthday, she reminded them about it in mischievous ways. Every time Grandfather tried to light his pipe, she blew the match out! If Camilla was playing marbles she hid one under the chair! When Mummy came in with biscuits, the little angel snatched one. Tibby, the cat, could see her, but she was invisible to the others.

'It must be little angel's birthday,' Mummy sighed. 'I'll bake her a cake!'

The tricks stopped, and peace reigned!

16 December
A wet day

Puddy the tabby cat hated getting wet! So when he saw the rain pouring down from dark grey clouds, he decided to find something interesting to do indoors, where he could keep dry.

He sat watching the goldfish blowing bubbles in their bowl. 'Poor things, wet all the time,' he miaowed. 'Wouldn't you like to come out for a while?'

We shall never know whether he really felt sorry for them, or whether he had a naughty plan in his head; for in his efforts to stretch up and hook his paw over the top of the bowl, he knocked the flower vase over, soaking himself with water! So Puddy got wet after all!

15 December
Kiddy's sleep

Kiddy, the young kangaroo, had to go into hospital to have her appendix out. Her parents took her, and she was put into a deep sleep so that she would know nothing about the operation.

It was soon over, and Kiddy was lying sleeping peacefully in her hospital bed with her parents sitting beside her.

Her mother held her hand. 'You can wake up now, Kiddy! You're quite all right, and Mummy and Daddy are here with you.'

Kiddy's eyelids flickered open, and closed again. 'I'm having such a lovely dream; I want to go on with it!' she murmured.

'You sleep as long as you like,' her mother whispered. 'Sleep is the best medicine!' They both crept away . . .

17 December
The legend of the polar bears

Once upon a time, long, long ago, all bears were dark brown.

A wicked magician was travelling round the world, and when he came to the North Pole he saw several dark brown bears walking about on the snow and ice.

'You can't stay here!' he shouted. 'You don't match the background.' He then used his magic powers to turn all the bears he could see into icebergs, which drifted away in the current.

But some of the bears he didn't see had time to cover themselves with snow, hoping that the magician would go away without noticing them. But he did notice them as he leaped and twirled around, looking for more brown bears.

'Aha! So you want to be white bears, do you?' he chuckled. 'Well then, you can stay as white bears!' And he scattered a magic fixing powder over them. They became polar bears, and have remained white ever since then!

18 December
The early lamb

What a surprise! Just a few days before Christmas, a lamb was born in the stable. Mary, the farmer's daughter, was very worried about the lamb, as it was born in the middle of winter instead of early spring, when lambs ought to be born. Its mother hadn't enough milk to feed her baby, and it got weaker and weaker.

Mary's mother helped her line a box with an old blanket, and they put it in the kitchen by the stove to make a warm bed for the lamb. Mary fed it with a baby's bottle full of warm cow's milk, and in a few days it was much stronger.

Soon it followed her wherever she went, and Mary took it for walks outside to get exercise, and grass to eat.

In the early spring the other lambs were born. Mary's lamb joined them in the meadow and gave them lessons in skipping!

19 December
Waiting for snow

It was the last day of school before the Christmas holidays, and Judy was feeling very excited. Her uncle, aunt and cousin Bobby were flying all the way from Australia to spend Christmas with her family! She had never met Bobby, but he had sent her a postcard saying he was swimming in the sea every weekend, and hoped it would snow during his visit.

Judy ran home. 'Do you think it's going to snow?' she asked her mother hopefully. 'Then I could take Bobby up the hill, and ride down on the toboggan, and we could build a big snowman, and have a snowball fight, and come in and eat roast chestnuts!'

'Well, let's hope it's not snowing when they fly in,' said Mummy. 'Planes can't land when the runways are very snowy.'

'Next year, I might spend Christmas Day on the beach, in Australia,' said Judy.

'If you're invited!' laughed Mummy.

20 December
The messenger

During the night a lot of snow fell. In the morning a sleepy marmot, who had curled up in a sheltered hollow under a bank, opened one eye, looked at the snowy scene around him, and quickly closed it again. 'I'll get up later,' he thought.

A few brave birds perched on trees, looking twice their usual size as they fluffed out their feathers to keep warm.

Then a strange figure came in sight, striding at great speed over the snow, though never leaving the faintest footprint. He was dressed all in blue, in a smart uniform with long boots, a peaked cap and warm white gloves.

'Who is that?' whispered the fawn.

'It's Father Christmas's messenger!' whispered the doe. 'He's checking that there's enough snow for his sledge to come this way on Christmas Eve!'

21 December
The magic carpet

Julian loved going to visit Aunt Agatha. She had travelled all over the world, and had collected many fascinating treasures.

She had strange-shaped beautiful shells displayed in cabinets, screens from China on which marvellous birds and flowers were painted, and a rug, covered with tiny mysterious designs, which made him think of faraway lands he might visit one day.

Julian lay on the little carpet one afternoon, looking at the patterns, when he felt himself floating up in the air, out through the window and over Aunt Agatha's vegetable patch! Down below was a tiny domed palace, nestling between the cabbages, and an Indian prince riding an elephant. Suddenly, a life-size worm wriggled towards the elephant, who reared up in fright, tipping the poor little prince on to the ground.

Julian couldn't help laughing! The worm must have seemed like a huge snake to the tiny elephant. But now he was inside again. Could it have been a dream?

22 December
Red and blue

'What shall I do this morning?' asked Blue Elf, reporting for duty at Father Christmas's toy factory.

'Take this box of Christmas tree decorations, streamers and dolls, and paint them blue,' he was told. When he reached the work bench, he found that Red Elf had arrived much earlier, and had already painted a boxful of decorations and toys red, and was on his second lot! Blue Elf couldn't stand red. While Red Elf was looking the other way, Blue Elf quickly painted over some of the red things; but as the red paint was still wet it mixed with the blue paint and made purple! Father Christmas came by to see how they were getting on.

'Splendid colour! Carry on!' he said.

23 December
Christmas decorations

'May I help to decorate the Christmas tree this year?' begged Cathy. Last year Mummy said she was too little, but this year she hoped to help.

'Yes! You're taller this year, and your hands are cleverer, so you can decorate the lower branches and I'll do the rest,' said Mummy. Cathy was thrilled!

First, they put blobs of cotton-wool on the branches to look like snow. Then Mummy took out the boxes of fragile glass balls and baubles, the coloured fairy lights, the silvery tinsel and glistening icicles, and they put them on the tree.

Cathy clapped her hands with delight. 'What do you think of the Christmas tree, Daddy?' she called. He turned from fixing a holly wreath on the door.

'It's prettier than last year,' he said, and a little cricket sitting by the hearth chirped in happy agreement.

24 December
Christmas Eve

It was Christmas Eve, and Angela had hung her red stocking at the end of her bed.

'It's a shame I've never had the chance to thank Father Christmas for his presents,' she said thoughtfully to her mother, as she went to bed. 'I've always been asleep when he's come!'

'I'm sure he understands.' Her mother kissed her, and left a candle burning.

'This time I'm *going* to stay awake,' she decided, and sat up very straight in bed, telling stories to her teddy bear.

But after a while she felt her eyelids drooping. 'I can't stay awake here; I'll have to sit on the floor by the fire.'

But all the excitement of the day and the late hour were too much for Angela, and she fell asleep there on the floor.

Later, she vaguely sensed quiet footsteps, and strong arms lifting her into bed . . . but she was too sleepy to open her eyes.

25 December
John's surprise

Although John had been given lots of lovely presents, the one he had hoped for most – a sleigh – was not among them.

'Oh well! I'll just have to wait for another Christmas,' he decided. 'I'll try out my new snow boots and hat, and take Rex for a walk in the forest.'

He set off, with his dog plunging bravely through the snow to fetch sticks.

Then he stopped and blinked hard, twice. It was hard to believe his eyes, for what he saw was a little pine tree, decorated with pretty coloured balls and shining tinsel! Most amazing of all was the sight of a fine sleigh, with a reindeer standing beside it! A label was tied to the sleigh, which read: Happy Christmas John! With love from all the animals.

He harnessed the deer and away they drove, through the snowy forest!

26 December
Suzy's new doll

Suzy had been such a good girl that Santa Claus had put a dear little golden-haired doll in her stocking. It looked rather like Suzy, and she called it Suzanna.

When Suzanna arrived in the toybox, Teddy and Soldier Boy looked admiringly at her, and introduced themselves.

Teddy tried to smooth his worn fur, and hide the patch on his waistcoat while smiling timidly at her. Soldier Boy was made of wood, and looked very smart indeed in his bright red painted uniform, black hat and boots, and gold braid and buttons. He stood up very straight and offered Suzanna his arm. She took it, and they went for a rather stiff stroll.

When they came back, she thanked him and sat down next to Teddy. 'He must be a very friendly bear to get so worn,' she thought, and slipped her arm through his.

27 December
Red Indians

Malcolm had been given a Red Indian outfit for Christmas, and he liked it so much he wore it all the time, even at mealtimes! In fact his mother had difficulty in persuading him to take if off when he went to bed.

Just now, there was silence – no war-cries, no bounding figure with plumed hat brandishing a rubber tomahawk.

'Has anyone seen my pipe?' said Grandfather. 'I thought I left it in the hall.'

'Malcolm's using it as a pipe of peace!' came Mandy's clear little voice. 'He's under the dining-room table.'

With a roar of rage, Big Chief Sitting Bull crawled out from under his wigwam, and chased Mandy upstairs into her bedroom, where he tried to tie her up with a dressing-gown cord. But she cried so loudly that Mother came, and said it was time Indians and squaws had their baths.

Didn't she know they washed in streams?

28 December
A winter coat

During the months of spring, summer and autumn. Mrs Stoat had been noticed wearing her smart reddish-brown coat, as she made her quiet, busy way around the fields and woodlands. Olly Owl had often seen her going hunting, and so had Rollo Rabbit – although he preferred to keep his distance when she was on the prowl.

One snowy day they saw an elegant lady, wearing a white fur coat, stalk by.

'Excuse me; who are you?' asked Olly.

'I'm Mrs Stoat, of course; don't you recognize me in my white ermine fur coat? The best people have *two* coats, you know!'

29 December
The old trunk

One day Bridget and Tony crept up into their grandmother's attic, while she was having a rest.

'Let's try and open this old trunk,' whispered Tony. They twiddled the knobs and fiddled with the catches until *snap*! A lock flew open, and they both heaved up the heavy lid. Inside were lots of lovely old-fashioned clothes, which they had great fun dressing up in.

Bridget was just reaching down to the bottom layer of clothes in the trunk, when she heard a thin, scratchy voice say 'Mamma! Mamma!'

She was frightened! 'Was that a ghost?' she asked Tony. He walked boldly over to the trunk and pulled out a talking doll!

Then Granny came in. 'Oh, thank you for finding Emily! I'd lost her,' she smiled.

236

30 December
The wood gnome

There's a little man living in the woods who is as old as the hills, as quick and as nimble as a squirrel and as mischievous as a monkey!

He wears a pine-cone for a hat, a waistcoat of moss, and boots of the finest toadstool skin. His cloak is a leaf, which changes colour with the season.

Now this little man tries to protect the woodlands from being spoiled by thoughtless people. So if he sees someone leaving litter, he puts ants in their sandwiches; or if ladies pick flowers, and take whole branches of flowering shrubs, or dig up plants, he hides their handbags, or tears their tights on thorns.

But he likes children! So if you're good he might show you secret paths to hidden places you've never seen before.

31 December
The mistletoe

Paddy, the dog, was most put out. For over a week now, the house had been full of decorations, with holly, gay paper chains and streamers, Christmas cards, and of course the tree itself; and Paddy's kennel wasn't decorated at all!

But Paddy's young masters had not forgotten him. On the last day of the year, they collected mistletoe from the woods, and hung a sprig over the entrance to Paddy's kennel. At midnight, they rushed out, woke him with shouts of 'Happy New Year, Paddy!' and gave him a big hug, right under his own bunch of mistletoe!